SILENT ELOQUENCE

SILENT ELOQUENCE

COLLECTION OF STORIES OF ORDINARY SOULS

SATYA MAYA

PARTRIDGE
A Penguin Company

Partridge books may be ordered through booksellers or by contacting:

Partridge India
Penguin Books India Pvt.Ltd
11, Community Centre, Panchsheel Park, New Delhi 110017
India
www.partridgepublishing.com
Phone: 000.800.10062.62

PREFACE

✝

Call them the Yin and Yang energies or the cosmic interplay of the eternal truth, *Satya* with its more visually overpowering and contextual rendering—*Maya,* that transcend the space to create the experience called the Universe and more so the earth in particular with its inhabitant humans, flora and fauna.

All stories emanate from the thought ensnared in the power of words. So the truth of thoughts is rendered in its contextual sense by the play of words. Central to all these is of course the human being—the experience. So when the Serpent, Apple, Adam and Eve all came together, stories started floating round is as much as the complimentary aspects and the biological distinctiveness of man and woman created difference in perceptions.

The male and female alter egos—Satya and Maya, come together to create Silent Eloquence as a collection of stories each distinct from the other. Spanning their own age difference and biological distinctions their collection puts forth the view point of the different ways in which a man and a woman express their innate thoughts on the vast canvas of words and collate them as stories for everyone to ponder.

Silent Eloquence comes in two distinct parts of Satya the male and Maya the female who through their own experience in their own ages see the same world differently and focus on the human relationship differently.

We hope the reader shall enjoy the unique experience of expressions that put the ordinary trivial happenings of life onto a larger canvas through observation and imagery.

Satya Maya

BOOK 1

Satya

"The face of truth is covered by a golden bowl. *Unveil it, O Pusan (Sun), so that I who have truth as my duty (satyadharma) may see it!*"

(Brhadaranyaka Upanisad)

CONTENTS

THE MIRRORED MYTHS

✢

"*B*ody of newborn girl found in the city drain. Head crushed. Police clueless"*, newspaper headlines screamed in bold letters calling attention.

Ramsingh's house wore a deserted look. The silence was palpable, made more eerie, from the gurgling sound from the hookah that Ramsingh sat smoking quietly, in the verandah. Behind the verandah, Roop Kanwar, Ramsingh's wife stared blankly on the wall of her dimly lit room. She no longer felt the pain of either the labor she had been through, barely twelve hours back, or the fact that her little infant had been taken away without her even getting a glimpse, never to come back. It was her third delivery and the second in succession to be lost to the so called code of honor of the house—*girls are forbidden to be born.*

Pride and honor weighed heavily over Ramsingh, more than the fact that it had been his own blood that had been shed out of his own whims on more than one occasion. He shoved the newspaper aside. Police had to be clueless. No one in his family dared to make a complaint of a missing child.

His gaze shifted to the purdah that swayed outside his wife's room. Remorseless that he was, he felt apathy for his estranged wife who had now "failed" him on more than one occasion. "Time to teach her a lesson", he mulled. Just then his father, the Thakur of his clan, called him, "Ramsingh, come here. I think we need to discuss your re-marriage plans. Your wife seems to be useless". The words echoed down the courtyard, into startled Roop Kanwar's ears, through the ajar door of her room. She tried to get up, but her weakness and unattended helplessness overcame her. Sobbingly, she collapsed back in her bed. Her four year old daughter, Ragini, her only surviving child, who had been spared her other siblings fate for being the first born, innocently watched her from behind the *purdah*. She had been told to be away from her mother since past couple of days. She awoke to a hushed silence that till a day before was full of expectation and a harried activity outside her mother's room. She could neither comprehend nor do anything about her mother's pathetic condition.

Roop Kanwar smiled weakly and beckoned, "Ragini! Come here child". Slowly, Ragini made her way to her mother's cot and immediately clung to her tightly. Roop Kanwar at once felt the longing and the sense of loneliness that her four year old little girl was suffering from the neglect by the family. She tried to throttle her emotions and swallowing a lump that had again formed in her throat, hugged her daughter with whatever energy she could muster.

"Both of us are going to be alone forever now," she silently told herself. She would soon be reduced to a servant in the house with the "new" wife coming in. That had been the tradition of this clan, since as long as she could remember her grand mother-in-law, narrate the stories.

Her husband Ramsingh was born into a land lord household whose authoritarian father had felt no need whatsoever for a formal education beyond class five for his son, which he thought was sufficient for ruling over the illiterate toilers that tilled his lands. Roop Kanwar came from a much poorer family and had been a brilliant student till her senior certification examination conducted by the board of education where she had done extremely well. She was then forced by her father's untimely demise and resultant poverty to discard any longing for more education. She loved to read and had great fancy for biological sciences. She remembered that the biological laws indicated that it was the human male chromosomes which determined the sex of the child to be born and not otherwise. "Alas, it is a pity that no one will ever understand the main reason for the birth of the girls in this household", she sighed, even as she held Ragini close. Her class lecturer's words echoed in her mind, "Science has proven beyond doubt that the chromosomal composition leans heavily in favor of the female in terms of being equal contributor to either sex as progeny, giving only "X" chromosomes. It is the male who is responsible for siring the female child specifically as he provided "X" or "Y", chromosomes. The combination of both the "X" chromosomes results in a girl whereas the combination of "XY" results in a boy. Yet the ignorance of this fact that thrives on lack of education amongst the majority of rural and urban population is always bliss for both pedagogues in creating a blame psychosis against the mother". Roop Kanwar was a living testimony to this. And she lived to suffer more for no fault of hers either by desire or by default.

Indian society has engendered the birth of boys for being symbols of continued lineage. Related to this is also the psyche that the salvation of the demised elders in a family is destined in the hands of the male progeny. Quite obviously therefore the desire for "fathering" a boy has always ruled supreme in India, till now. Yet this very burning desire of having a boy in every household has kindled the fires that India has witnessed for years as female infanticides. The other side of the coin remains in the special treatment given to the boy over the girl siblings without realization that the psyche of the discriminated girls gets scarred, perhaps forever. Ragini, in time too was to become a victim of this unjustified fancy.

There was no one Roop Kanwar could turn to. "Oh! Lord Krishna, please help us. What have I erred in to beget such misery? Will there ever be any hope for me", she sobbed silently, with Ragini still clinging to her.

Hope however is what God created the human's for. It is only because of the hope of the possibilities and the yearning for knowing more that the human race has surmounted the animal and plant kingdoms to rule the planet. It was as if by divine intervention to Roop Kanwar's prayers, that the phone in the verandah rang, harshly enough to break the lingering silence. "Hello", Ramsingh answered in his bellicose voice. His voice suddenly changed to respectful whimper "Uncle, Many Pardons. I am sorry I was a little busy", he lied. "Yes!Yes! He is here. I'll just give the phone to him," as Ramsingh passed on the phone to his father who had summoned him a short while ago. It was Ramsingh's uncle, his father's elder brother and a doctor of international repute who had after revolting against his family tradition taken up medical studies and had settled abroad. Ramsingh's father respected his elder brother and was also awed by his powerful persona. After a while Ramsingh's father put the phone down and announced in a much lighter mood, "He is coming next week. That's good. Let him go. We shall then discuss and finalize the proposal for your remarriage. So many of our clansmen, are ready to give their able daughter's hand in yours. Here are some photographs. Have a look and tell me later on! I am getting old and more and more concerned about my lineage, you being the only son I have", he said getting up and leaving Ramsingh to ponder over an envelope containing photographs of girls who were being offered to him for being his second wife.

Roop Kanwar heaved a sigh of relief. She had earned some respite till Dr. Karansingh's visit was over. She recalled her earlier chance to meet Dr. Karansingh just a few months after her marriage. She had then impressed him with her knowledge and aptitude for the biological sciences one day.

Traditional households prohibit the females to meet the elder male members openly. But that evening was somewhat different. Preparations were on for welcoming Dr. Karansingh, who was arriving the next day. Humid Monsoon had set in and the perspiring male members were enjoying a siesta amidst the trees in the courtyard. It so happened that a snake bit one of the male attendants sitting on the ground near Ramsingh's father cot. Everyone was suddenly gripped in panic as the snake was identified to be a poisonous one.

On hearing the hue and cry, Roop Kanwar, remembering her first aid training at school, ran across with a small rope and knife, unmindful of her father in law's presence. She had then cut open the wound to let blood flow from the patient's leg and tied the rope tightly above the wound. The man was shifted for medical treatment and was soon out of danger. A life saved by quick presence of mind. Roop Kanwar's had become known in the neighborhood for her bravery and quick thinking, though her archaic in-laws looked upon her with disdain for having broken the *purdah*. The next day when Dr. Karansingh came to know of the brave deed from the villagers, he summoned her and asked her about the episode and how she knew what to do. She had from behind her veil recounted the story along with her own interest in biological sciences and the first aid training she had received at school. "*Bahurani*, I am really proud of you! God Bess You", he had said.

Roop Kanwar now saw hope in the news that Dr. Karansingh's visit was at a time when she needed help—to fight injustice that was being done to her and her innocent daughter; to fight the inept thinking of the household; to fight the ignorance and the customs built on such ignorance that had cost the lives of many a girl child. She knew Dr. Karansingh would be furious to know about the multiple infanticides in his own brother's home, but someone had to make him aware of this. She also knew that his father in law would even order her killed if he ever knew her thoughts, but then it was better to die once fighting for a righteous cause than virtually die cowardly day after day under misery and humiliation from one's own family members. "He needs to be told. But how?" she started thinking furiously, her tears forgotten. A ray of hope it was. Her prayers seemingly answered.

Ragini had quietly slept off in her lap in the meantime. The look of contentment on her face and an innocent smile brought Roop Kanwar back in the present. She gently lay her daughter down on the bed beside her and caressed Ragini's forehead. The atmosphere in the room turned from turmoil to tranquility in the shadow of the unspoken bond between the mother and her child.

Just then she heard Ramsingh clear his throat from behind the ajar door indicating he wanted to say something. "Uncle Karansingh*ji* is expected next week. I want you to be ready and behave normally," he curtly ordered and left. She started thinking again when an idea struck her. She thought over and soon a plan was ready in her mind. She now had the advantage of her forced seclusion for gaining strength as well as fine tuning her idea that would save her and her daughter's life. Roop Kanwar was patiently reviewing her plan each day and was extremely confident of executing it to her advantage. Time had come to break the mirrored myths once and forever, which the generations had been blindly passing on as their own reflections without bothering to stop and examine their truth.

Dr. Karansingh was coming the next day. The preparations in the household were on. She had been temporarily granted the grace period with all the family members behaving cordially with her, at least in public view. Then the day came when Dr. Karansingh arrived. A special room had been laid out for him with thrust on making his stay as comfortable and close to his western tastes as possible. Roop Kanwar's father in law knew that his daughter in law was liked by his elder brother and so for once he overcame his ego to allow her to supervise Dr. Karansingh's room personally, exactly what she had hoped for. Dr. Karansingh had a fancy of reading newspapers with his early morning tea in the verandah. Roop Kanwar knew of this and it fitted perfectly into her plan for survival. The day before on pretext of getting some special linen and towels from Ramsingh's room, her own old bedroom till few days ago, she had siphoned off the envelope containing photographs of the girls, one of whom was to be the chosen one to be her husband's consort, to beget him sons, which she was being blamed to have failed. She carefully folded the towels and linen in the cupboard and inserted the envelope in between so neatly that no sooner an effort was made to pick up the towel or linen, the envelope would fall down in full view of Dr. Karansingh, who she had hoped would certainly examine the contents and ask searching questions from his brother to know the truth. It was her only chance of survival and her plan.

The next morning, she had expected scenes to be enacted by the various actors she had imagined in her plan. Nothing happened. Dr. Karansingh quietly sipped his morning tea even as he read the news papers. Roop Kanwar's heart sank. She had lost. Her plan had failed. It was the end of the road for her with the dungeons of monotony and the pain of seeing her husband with his consort day in and day out. She cried internally and continued quietly with the chores behind her veil. Soon Dr. Karansingh got up and went out for a walk to his old friends in the neighborhood. Roop Kanwar, dashed inside his room for cleaning away the tea pot. She looked around and saw the towel hung on the stand. Then she turned and opened the cupboard and rummaged to locate the envelope. It was not there. "More trouble! Had someone else found the envelope and taken it away? Now What? Surely my father-in-law is going to kill me. Oh God! What will happen to young Ragini? Oh! Why did I rush into something so stupid without thinking of her?" as many questions as the incessant tear drops that flowed down her cheeks, blissfully invisible to anyone from behind her customary veil.

The day ended uneventfully, but the pangs of a lost cause seemed to haunt her continuously nagging her conscience. The next day and the next one also passed with more relatives and friends coming in to meet Dr. Karansingh. Roop Kanwar was now becoming more restless with each passing day for in just another two days it will all be over for both mother and daughter. They would be confounded to a hell on earth for no fault of their and that too without recourse.

But hope is a silver lining in the clouds. "Bahurani, come here", Dr. Karansingh called her that evening. Roop Kanwar was stunned. These were the first words that Dr. Karansingh had spoken to her since he arrived. Slowly she made her way into the room and respectfully bowed to the elder in the customary way, bending almost double with folded hands. "Tell me the truth and nothing but the truth", he said even as she looked down upon her toes through the veil, trembling in trepidation. "Tell me what's going on in this house?" She was taken aback. "Come on, I want to know", he said throwing the envelope in front of her on a little peg table, while sitting down on the sofa opposite her. "What is this? Who are these girls? What are these photographs doing here in this house?" he fired a salvo of questions. "Tell me is something wrong with Ramsingh or you for that matter?" he continued without waiting for her answer, as if he already knew something.

Roop Kanwar stood still, tears in her eyes. She was quiet. This was the moment she had been waiting for and praying all these days but now she could not muster enough courage to speak her heart out. "*Hukum* . . .", she stuttered incoherently. Just then Ramsingh and his father entered the room and sat beside Dr. Karansingh, followed by Thakur Rampal, Dr. Karansingh's school mate and a respected member of their clan.

Suddenly Dr. Karansingh turned to Thakur Rampal and asked him "Do you know her?" he said pointing to Roop Kanwar. "Yes. I do know Bahurani. Why?", Thakur Rampal replied calmly. "Why?" bellowed Dr. Karansingh, "Why then you have made an offer of marrying your daughter to Ramsingh?" The silence that followed was deafening. Roop Kanwar's heart pounded so fiercely that she felt it would pop out of her bosom. She trembled in fear. Ramsingh and his father were dumbfounded. "How in the heavens did Dr. Karansingh knew about this?" Ramsingh's father was furiously thinking. Even as he knew what was coming next, Dr. Karansingh turned to Ramsingh and bellowed, "So tell me what's wrong with Bahurani, that you want another wife? What is it that you want from her? Boys? Is that it? Do you know how one gets sons or who is responsible for producing sons"? Ramsingh stood speechless and ashen faced. He could not utter a word except staring blankly at nowhere in the room. He could not muster enough courage to look into Dr. Karansingh's furious eyes.

Dr. Karansingh now turned to his brother and said, "Do you know that it is always the male who is responsible for producing either a girl or a boy? Well even a school going child knows from his basics in biology that it is the chromosome from the father that determines the sex of the child to be born and not otherwise. So, if anyone has failed to give you a grandson, don't blame Bahurani. It is your own son who is responsible not by any design but as a matter of chance. Do you still want him to remarry? And don't ask me how I know about what goes in this house. No one has bothered to even tell me. But I know of both the sad episodes that you have caused with your ignorance to this household and perhaps more to Bahurani. It is a shame that I learnt it by sheer chance of someone correlating the newspaper items with the stoic silence you have been maintaining in public, when everyone knew about Bahurani's condition of becoming a mother again two times in past three years. Since you did never bother to share any good news with me I had to come personally to see the truth myself. The day I saw Rampal's daughter's photograph in this envelope, my doubts were confirmed and I had confront all three of you for the great injustice that you all were planning to execute to both Bahurani and Rampal's daughter. It was clear that your ignorance would cause further damage to more families. What if Rampal's daughter too would have delivered a girl? You would have remarried Ramsingh again, a third time, isn't it? Shame on you! Have you ever thought that if everyone starts killing infant girls like you do, there will not be any women left to sustain human generation? Have you forgotten that we too have been born out of a female? Even Bahurani knows this much science, isn't it?"

Having spent his pent up anger on his brother Dr. Karansingh stopped for a glass of water. That one moment break was perhaps enough for catharsis to take over the father son duo as they broke down sobbing like children. "We are sorry. We didn't know the truth. Our crimes are unpardonable". Thakur Rampal too was speechless. He had lost his entire dignity in front of his old schoolmate. With eyes downcast, they were all silently cursing their own ignorance and lack of knowledge.

Perhaps for the first time it had dawned on Ramsingh what education really meant. He was at once filled with remorse and melancholy, for the damage he had caused to his own family and more so to his wife, who had borne the pain without ever complaining. He suddenly remembered his little daughter Ragini and for the first time his heart went out to her. He got up with a start, walked out from the room and was back holding a smiling Ragini in his arms.

Roop Kanwar had won. Her hope for the rightful place for her daughter and her own self had been acknowledged with grace. She bent forwarded and touched Dr. Karansingh's feet in gratitude. This time the tear drops were full of happiness. She thanked God for being kind enough to hear her prayers for she knew that majority of the females facing similar predicament were hardly as lucky. "When will the generation learn to respect gender equality?" the question left her nagging, even as she made her way slowly out of the room, leaving Ragini happily play with her father and grandfather. The mirrored myths lay forever shattered, at least in her household, but it had taken the pain of countless unshed tears by the mother in agony for the two dead innocent infants who fell to their own father's presumptuous beliefs.

IN SEARCH OF SOLACE

✠

The Hindu culture has over the centuries mutated into myriad forms of mores and customs. Some of these, bank upon the pure ignorance of the masses while some other have graduated into educated homes based on the superstitions imbibed into daily life with studied élan to find ways of solace to troubled minds in times of turmoil.

It was on Wednesday, 9th November, 2011, that the conclusion was foregone. It was a matter of time, that mother would rest in peace forever. The struggle between life and death in the battlefield of a modern fully equipped Intensive Care Unit continued though, unabated.

Tense moments had become days of anxiety. Three dialysis across, the doctors themselves had all, but given hope, and worked in servitude to their pledge to the profession.

Suffering, increased beyond bearing for the family, what to say of mother herself lying needled to the bed, much akin to *Bhishma Pitamaha* in the great Indian epic, *The Mahabharata*. She had herself lost much confidence with each long day and the inventory turnover of co-patients bidding goodbye forever.

Prayer and treatment go hand in hand with each complimenting the other in such times. It was no different in this case either. I talked to a gentle soothsayer who had earlier responded with positivity in times of trouble. "Son", he said, "There is nothing one can do against the will of God. What has to happen will happen and it is even known to you scientifically or otherwise. Yet, the suffering can be reduced. Go and feed the poor. Give fodder to cows and pray. God willing solace will be there".

It was a mission I had to take with all the pain and helplessness. I mustered courage to find eatables and fruits from nearby vendors and went out to locate the poor—a task not much difficult. People advised, "Go to *Lord Ganesha* temple. Today is Wednesday and there will be plenty around."

Yet, I chose another route. Wednesday, in any case is feasting time for the poor. For there are hundreds of devotees doing their sharing that is stuffed in the destitute "safes". So, instead, I landed on the roadside rag pickers where the women and children soon made a bee line surrounding me for whatever I had to offer. My wife sat in the car taking small packs of food out to be given to each little hand with expectant eyes for the share. The food was soon over but the hunger remained insatiable. Was this the solace that the soothsayer wanted me to experience? The levels of suffering are personal and can only be reduced if you compare with the worse.

My next mission was to feed the cows. It was late in the evening and so the fodder was neither available nor were the cows to be seen. So I decided to complete the activity next day and arranged for purchase of green fodder early next morning.

Back in the hospital mother continued to suffer, as I settled for the night on the waiting hall bench with frequent lookouts on mothers condition. Despite Oxygen support her breathing had deteriorated, heart beats registered uneasy jumps and falls and she showed spasmodic movements of the entire body in agony, which was even more agonizing to watch. Her eyes were half open and I could feel the urge in them to speak but no strength left to act. I wept as I had done many times in the loneliness of solitude. My wife always stood there with me each night sharing the grief.

Early next morning, I started with the fodder to feed the cows in the Goshala maintained by the Government. Feeding numerous cows was an experience in the chill of early morning in November. They jostled with each other for fresh food and many were sidelined. The meek expressions in their eyes did not get unnoticed and I along with my wife went on spreading the fodder to the distant and desolate cows. The cows fed happily and for once I felt a sense of calm spreading. Was this the solace I was searching?

My wife and I decided to make a visit to the Missionaries for Charity, Mother Teresa's incomparable mission of helping the destitute, selflessly. We took food packets for the inmates in cartons along with fruits, which were gracefully acknowledged.

It was almost seven thirty in the evening. We returned back to the hospital. Mother was still the same and it looked another night of vigil and wait. I stood next to her for half an hour and went out praying to God to give her peace. Barely minutes later, ICU doctor summoned us inside. Mother had chosen to depart and there she was gasping with decreasing intensity and a serene calm descending gradually on her face, as if she intended to sleep after a long tiring journey.

It was all over on the night of Thursday, 10th November, 2011. Soothsayer had made me believe that the suffering was reduced. It could be a coincidence or much more, that indeed even as I accomplished the task of feeding the poor and the cows, mother had perhaps found her solace.

THE LAST RITES

✝

I lit the pyre. Encompassed in it was the body that had carried my mother since her birth eighty two not so long years ago. It was soon to be destroyed, for mother had already chosen to find another life.

Birth and death are a cyclical phenomenon. But, in every socio-religious group, the detailed customs that encompass the death of a human being find stricter adherence than the ones concerned with a new birth. In the Hindu culture, with the stress on the purifying aspect of cremation by fire, even if one tries to think out of the archaic systems by focusing on the more burning issues of depleting availability of pyre-wood, pollution, hygiene and cleanliness, the flow of emotional fuel will in all certainty burn out all such logic.

The wood soon caught fire and with it emanated the crackling of bones, releasing the trapped gases in the joints. Tears welled again in my eyes. I had the least time to know mother, being the youngest. Mother had raised her own younger brothers and sisters since a tender age of fifteen when she lost her mother. So all of them were more like her own children and all revered this fact.

From times immemorial the birth and death processes have been institutionalized by the various civilizations that spawned on the earth. Each incorporated the traditions and customs to weave into a fabric that has come to be called as culture in the more erudite circles. Both the natural cycles of birth and death have been recast into social patterns of acceptability that normally would defy any logical reasoning. These are the matters where heart rules supreme over the head—emotions over reasoning.

In this entire milieu, a whole lot of lives depend on making a living. Strange but true, even the dead body has its value in making whole business streams flourish like the specialized ambulances, pundits, pyre wood choppers, bamboo, cloth and so many other merchants. Specialized shops with all under one roof services are the norm of the day.

Soon, the pyre was ablaze with maddening alacrity and with the plume of smoke filling the shed and nothing else to do but wait for the *katya pandit*, as he was called, for conducting fresh set of rituals, my mind filled with natural remorse, took me down the recent happening since her demise.

The ambulance had delivered the dead body, late in the night and we lay her to sleep on the bed set up on the ground. For sleeping she was with a deep calm settled on her face after a long drawn battle with her own self from multiple organ failure. It had started with a very pithy remark a month ago when she had candidly stated "I do not want to live now. It is extremely laborious", even as I touched her feet while leaving for work.

Ice slabs, arranged as if from nowhere at that hour by my co-brother, were brought in to delay the biological actions on a lifeless body till the eventual cremation. All of us had passed a sleepless night sitting around and taking breaks for stretching the limbs that ached on the hard ground in the vicinity of ice slabs. The only source of heat, were the incense sticks billowing weak streams of fragrance keeping the sense of freshness alive.

First light saw hectic activity for locating the venue for cremation. It was ultimately decided after deliberation to go where others from family had gone earlier. Thanks to the modern transportation, the transshipment has become easier than the actual ritual of carrying the deceased on the shoulders till cremation. Cremation grounds were created as a necessity in the vicinity of households. However, the spawning cities have all but distanced them from the nearness to communities in general. Natural consequence has been the mechanized attitude towards what had once been a most sacred rite.

Well, nothing can be done without the ubiquitous pundit who has to ultimately supervise the activity like master of ceremonies. He soon descended after little follow up and immediately was in an incessant hurry to get over the business apart from collection of service charges and free donation. Pain for one is gain for other. Nothing can more exemplify this. But then this is what life is all about.

Even as the ladies of the household bathed and dressed the body for the one last time, the pundit started firing instructions in multitasking mode. I was directed to the barber in waiting for the ceremonial tonsure that was soon under way. *Kusha (dry grass)* was soaked, for making rings for me to wear and balls of flour called *pindas (wheat balls)* were soon prepared by pundit with other ingredients, I could hardly recollect through my remorse.

He soon rushed me to take bath and instructed me to dress up in the brand new clothes of cotton and rubber slippers bought in especially by the team deputed in the wee hours. I still marvel how they got the clothes so early. These clothes were to be daily washed and worn daily till the whole period of mourning, ten days to be precise, was over. As was expected, the clothes shrunk with each wash and were soon three quarter their original size, making me to struggle through them each morning.

In the meanwhile the ordered goods at the cremation ground for carrying mother on her last journey as a mortal arrived along with the vehicle that was the transport. I couldn't be a part of the ceremony being the one for the major work. However, I do recall from experience of shouldering the responsibility in case of many relatives where I had to do the preparation. The *baikunthi* as the carriage is called was decked up in red, my mother having left the world in a married state. She was in accordance covered in red sheet and covered with flowers. The *baikunthi* was decked up with metal *ghantis (small brass utensils)* that jingled on the movement like bells.

Having bathed and dressed as directed, it was now my turn to join the others. Pundit ji directed me to sit besides mother and after some fast recital of umpteen *shlokas* asked me to place one of the *pindas* prepared near the head in the *baikunthi*. I still do not comprehend the significance, nor was there anyone who could reason it out. Thereafter, started the process, of laying garlands and taking four rounds each by the family members and relatives. With so many people around joining the queue, the small area around was packed with no scope for the queue to inch forward. Eventually saner counsel prevailed and people started moving in a concentric manner to complete their rounds. Pundit ji as usual was impatient and kept exhorting the people to deposit their regards at the feet, soon to be pocketed by him. He then made me lay a coconut at the feet which eventually would be used later on in the cremation ground.

No sooner I had put the coconut as directed, it was picked up and kept aside. The *baikunthi* was lifted up amongst heart rendering chants of "*Ram Naam Satya Hai*" and with feet pointing to the door left the room with mother, on me and my cousins' shoulders. We stopped again at the main gate and pundit ji repeated the ritual of placing the second *pinda* near the arms. We walked a hundred yards to a nearby crossing where the transport waited. Pundit ji rushed through the ritual and asked me to place the third *pinda* near the knees.

Leaving some of the weeping ladies behind I sat in the van with mother's *baikunthi* nearby on the bench. Father occupied the co-driver's seat and two more persons sat near for holding the *baikunthi*. We started the last journey with mother. Accompanying us on a bike was the barber holding a mud pot hung by coir rope carrying *kande*—smoking pieces of dried cow dung that were to be used for generating fire for lighting up the pyre later. Others soon followed in procession.

Half an hour later we reached the destination—the outskirts of cremation ground. The *baikunthi* was laid to rest for the final time and pundit ji soon got over the ritual of placing the fourth *pinda* near mother's feet. I took a round of the body walking backwards with a pot of water in my hands dripping down. I soon poured the entire water at the feet and called my mother aloud.

We soon formed the foot procession again and ferried the *baikunthi* to the pyre prepared by now in part. The *pindas* were now removed from the *baikunthi* as were the shawl and red cloth covering the body over the clothes dressed up after final bath at home. The body was shifted to the pyre. *Ghee* was poured all across along with sandalwood powder and other *hawan samagri* that would eventually help in burning of the body. More wood was piled up and soon it was time. The smoking *kandas* were put on thatch which with a practiced swinging action by the *katya pandit* caught the wind and alighted. The pyre was now ready to be lit. I walked around the unlit pyre with the raging thatch in my hands and placed it at the feet to light up the pyre. I called out aloud to mother for one last time. Tears ran uncontrollably.

I was brough back from my thoughts to the present. *Katya pundit* had just called out. "Please come for *Kapal Kriya*". *Kapal Kriya* is the breaking of skull which otherwise does not break in pieces. A bamboo was split by striking against the ground. The coconut, placed earlier at mother's feet was fixed in the split and with ghee pouring on it was used as the spear to break the skull, visible through the haze of raging fire. It was hot and scorching and a gentle nudge was all that was required. With the bamboo I drew out lord Rama's name on the ground at the feet of the pyre and prayed one last time for mother's peace.

Now it was turn of the people who had been part of the procession to offer pieces of *chhana or kandas*—pieces of dried cow dung as the last ritual for the day, before I finally offered the same.

Early next morning I was back at the cremation ground, in my shrunk clothes. The smoldering pyre was rummaged for picking pieces of undestroyed bones, washing them with water, curd, milk, honey, *itra* (scent) and *ghee* and collecting them in a red cloth before eventually depositing them in the Holy waters of Pushkar Sarovar, the next day, a ritual which I was not allowed for some strange reason to personally attend, being left out to be at home with the memories of mother and the last rites.

THE PLATONIC LUSTS

✠

1

The overcast sky lit up with lightening. The usual loud rapport of thunder clap followed. Rain drops began to fall in gay abandon, as if competing for a "me-first" collision with the earth. Nitya remained unmoved. Holding the railing of her balcony, she continued to stare in the dark, above the buildings nearby. Her tears subtly concealed in the rain.

For many, perhaps it was just another day. For Nitya, it was one day she longed for, from the core of her heart. Yet today it was ending washed up with just the reminiscence of the times bygone. Even this evanescence was overpowering. Shrey had not been able to make it for their twentieth wedding anniversary, second time in succession from his place of work. These two long years of forced separation, balancing the family needs with the means to meet them had cast toll on their earlier eighteen years of blissful coexistence. True, time changes and the lost moments can never be relived, but the associated lingering is independent of such logic and it takes great effort to control such random thoughts that just run amok. Always portrayed as the made for each other couple, they had been envy to many. But that had been till two years ago.

So, it was Nitya's overflowing emotions that now clouded all reasoning. Her heart ruled over the mind—as it always did at such times. The parcel Shrey had so lovingly sent lay open on her table. It was a beautiful dress. Shrey must have spent considerable time in finding this for her. She knew it. "He's so particular about my preferences", she thought. Yet some thorn pricked her deep. It was the beautifully manuscript letter enclosed in the parcel. His wishes so well articulated in poetic meter, as always. All was a dream come true, a balm to reduce the pain of his absence. Yet the last line, in the PS note pinched her. "Sweetheart! The moment you get the dress please put on and send me your photograph. I'm dying to see you wearing it! And Guess what, I had to take Kavya along for locating this exclusive shop for this dress."

Thunderclap again! And though the sound was inaudible to her, it brought young Akuj running out to her. "Mamma, come in. You are getting wet. There's no light. I'm scared", he tugged. Reality broke her chain of thoughts. Wiping her tears under the camouflage of rainwater, she smiled weakly and turned to go inside holding Akuj's little palm tightly. Akshita, her elder progeny was stoic in her silence, unusual for her teens. She had just grown up beyond her years.

2

"The meeting is scheduled at 11. Please see the presentation slides. I've modified the same as advised by you. Call me up in case you need anything else". Kaavya.

The ubiquitous *'post it'* label pasted on the desktop monitor was audibly visible. Shrey could literally hear his subordinate's message. He had barely finished reading the hard copies of the presentation slides that lay in front of his monitor when suddenly a bubbling, energetic enigma entered his cabin, without any presumptions. "Morning Sir", Kaavya said, just as Shrey looked up from his papers. "Happy Anniversary! How's Nitya Ma'm? Did she like the dress? I'm sure she did? It's so beautiful! Isn't it?" Kaavya stated all in a breath, before Shrey could even wink. "Thanks, Thanks! No, I've still to get the feedback on the dress. I'm pre-occupied with the presentation and of course I'm terribly upset because of this meeting colliding with the most awaited day of our married life." Shrey replied even while reading the handouts. "Anyway, could you please provide me the backup papers also; Here's what I need", he said while handing over a small slip, without even bothering to look up at her. Kaavya stood for a brief moment and then quietly slipped out. She had now known Shrey long enough for the past two years to understand his ability to focus on the immediate and hiding anything that was going on at the back of his mind. She could feel a sense of sadness in his otherwise calm voice, perhaps covered under the pretext of urgency. His resentment of living a separated life was not completely unknown to her. He had shared, as he did with many others, in general, the circumstances that had forced him and Nitya to live a life, which was separated by just over four hundred kilometers of distance, but which could be breached by neither of them frequently because of the split responsibility of earning a sustenance for him and taking care of the family—old parents and young children, for her. She pondered briefly, then shrugged and got on with her work.

Time flew, as it always does when you are burdened with heaps of work that suddenly tends to overwhelm, especially on a Monday, the blues notwithstanding. Kaavya pushed back her chair from work station and redid her hair clip, an act that always accentuated her lithe body much to the envy of her female colleagues and sighs for the other sex. She surmised the morning events as she set back for a breather over a cup of tea, served routinely each day, providing a break for recollecting her thoughts. It wasn't in particular that an older man, that too, a much married one, attracted her over her own age group. But surely there was some other worldly charm that constantly drifted her thoughts to Shrey. At first it had been simply out of awe for being associated with a superior who was dreaded in discourse for being upright and a no nonsense go getter—"Such a hardnosed snob", she had thought then! Almost double her age, but appearing much younger, youthful and always impeccably dressed day after day with complete knowledge about almost everything on or off job, was what she found Shrey to be—not so snobbish after all. He was pleasant to talk to and never ever gave a chance to gossip. She flashed back her thoughts to her last birthday when quite surprisingly Shrey gave her a small gift. Basic curtsey, that is now-a-days a norm for the superiors to build bridges with their subordinates. But that little gesture had moved her immensely. Perhaps her own pre-meditated thoughts about the "hard nose" had suddenly evaporated and she had been caught off-guard. Respect had replaced skepticism and perhaps a new bond forged, inexplicable in any manner, not congruent to any defined relationship. It was something beyond the classical form of attraction or office romance. It was much deeper, and without any expectations or nuance. Both of them perhaps shared a similar feeling but none would ever say. Shrey of course was much more sensible and gentleman enough for not fanning the cupid flames that come so easy with young age. For him, perhaps, it was a tacit and a very mature understanding that was at once difficult to define or enclose in a relationship. Pure! Platonic! Without any lust! A concept difficult to understand in today's material world.

Kaavya suddenly felt a lump in her throat, same as she had felt on receiving the gift, and which had subsequently opened up a vent of tears through the better part of night. She cleared her throat and went back to work with a sigh. Her mobile was vibrating. It was Ranvir, her boyfriend for four years from Chennai. She responded the call, "Hi! Whats up?" "Where the hell are you? I have been calling you up for long now", Ranvir said. "Oh! Just busy as usual in some work", she lied and immediately felt the bitter taste in mouth. 'How could she lie to her boy friend, with whom she was planning to get married after a time tested courtship? What was it that was bothering her? Was it Shrey? But he had never ever been flirtatious with her. Why then was she feeling so diffident?'

She cleared her throat, "Actually boss is in some important meeting and some presentations, backup and the usual gamut to foot. Sorry, could not respond! What's the plan? When are you coming down? I need to discuss something serious about our lives", she said. "Wow! At Last! My prayers are answered!" Ranvir was ecstatic, "Shall I start just now?" he teased. "Oh! Come On! Don't start it all over again! I seriously need some help about the plans for my MBA program. Remember, you had promised me that I will be allowed a boon! One last year of old college life, before we settle down", Kaavya pleaded with all her drooling sweetness. "Swetheart! You know, I just can't ignore your mesmerizing commands. But seriously, can we not give our relationship a break for maturing earlier than your planned sojourn?" Ranvir mimicked, "It's been ages since we discussed something better than your MBA. I know it is important for you. But can we really not switch the years of study with our marriage? After all what difference will it make? Together we can really plan a much more flexible plan for your studies. And off course you will be better off without about your 'hard nose' boss, who in any case you have to leave once you prepare for your studies."

Kaavya was quiet for a moment. "Ranvir, I! . . . Hey! I'll call you back in the evening. Something urgent came up. Bye", she hurriedly hung up. The office peon was standing before her waiving a small piece of paper. "Madam Please rush. You are required inside. Boss is waiting. And please see this slip".

"God I'm going crazy" she muttered under her breath, "What's happening? The guy is driving me mad. Now what?" she looked up at the slip even while scurrying towards the conference hall, stopping for a while to pick up the sheaf of papers listed in the small slip in her hands.

Thoughts collided again and not surprisingly Shrey was again floating freely with them. She actually longed for the moment to be face to face with Shrey, so much for her feigned cursing for his intervening officially during her private calls.

She knocked and entered the conference room. "Good noon Sir", she said as she handed the sheaf to Shrey, who was chairing the meeting. "Sit, Sit", Shrey gestured. "Actually we just received an urgent message from the Board. You are being recommended to attend a top level meeting at Chennai, tomorrow that is; in my place of course. So pack your bags and start right now. Tickets are at reception", Shrey said with a slight smile. She caught the amusement in Shrey's voice. She knew that he knew about Ranvir being in Chennai. At once she felt ecstasy and a pang. Ecstasy, of seeing Ranvir, after a long time, to whom, she had been talking moments ago, was understandable. But, the pang of leaving Shrey behind, and not seeing him for some days was inexplicable. Was it love? Was she romantically inclined towards Shrey? Was she not betraying Ranvir? How could she feel attracted to a much married older man and at the same time feel happy about meeting her boyfriend of years? No one answered these questions as her head thumped with each thought jumping to grab her attention. The muddling thoughts enervated her as she quietly walked back in small steps.

Four hours later, she was airborne to Chennai on a long flight. Enough time to attend to her wild thoughts now that even the nagging mobile was also statutorily switched off for in flight safety.

Shrey returned in her thoughts. "It is so difficult not to think about you. Where have you transcended from in my life? And why can't you be any younger by years to be by my side? Why the hell I keep on returning back to you in my thoughts? Oh! What a mess!" she silently sighed looking out at nowhere in the vast expanse of evening sky lit by the setting sun. Below the earth rushed by with all its meandering rivers and the winding roads, perhaps much akin to her thoughts. Any other day she would have happily gazed at the beauty of nature that spread its arms beckoning her. Not today. Today the pang was overwhelming. So it was love after all, but one sided. "Shrey's a loving husband of an exceptionally graceful wife and a caring father of two beautiful children. What will he say?" she sighed and closed her eyes, but could not sleep. Closed eyes now provided her thoughts a much bigger canvas to let her relive the scenes from her not so recent past. Her mind drifted to the various educative mobile messages that Shrey had shared deliberately with her, as perhaps he had with many others. Some of them in prose while some others in pure poetic form that simply touched a chord deep within. Shrey had a gift for penning verse and prose with equal dexterity and some of his renderings were beyond this world. It was this clarity of perception that had endeared him to her so much so that she found herself in the present situation.

Kaavya squirmed in her seat to adjust her posture and in the brief interlude her thoughts shifted. Shrey was fond of her. It was obvious for he had shared so many things with her that perhaps few others knew. But it was also a fact that any talk that crossed between them was in the knowledge of Nitya, an example of what trust between devoted couples meant. Shrey would never ever keep a secret from

Nitya and Kaavya was no exception. This was perhaps the distinction in the perceived relationship between the two of them—while she perhaps had confided in none about how she felt for Shrey, he had never given second thoughts about what he said to her. Maybe this was the age difference or the experience that made him more resolute to cover up emotions. May be that he was aware of her feelings but never openly acknowledged so. She remembered once while ferrying her back from office in his car he had candidly stated "Look Kaavya, there is an invisibly thin curtain of modesty that separates emotions from reality. Between us, Call it age difference or call it official decorum, it is my duty to maintain this sanctity at all times, for your own sake". So it was amply clear to her that while he understood her emotions, for him there was never a chance of this relationship going deeper on the physical front. It had to be a much different but extremely difficult type of relationship for her though, one that had actually started nagging her with enough potential for guilt and imagination for reading between the lines for everything that happened or did not happen between them.

The plane had begun to descend. Life is such a trial especially for emotionally sensitive persons. People who think through their hearts are seldom the ones who remain calm and unaffected by what happens around them. Kaavya, like Shrey was one of these kinds and obviously had overloaded her heart with emotions. Being grown up endows one with myriad experience. However, it doesn't mean that they become capable of handling emotions with the maturity required, a virtue that comes only with trust and commitment. Kaavya was now in a quagmire of sorts with her heart aching for two souls, one of whom could not ever be logically her soul mate but her heart would have none of that logic.

She struggled to come out of her entangling thoughts and tried to put up a smiling and eager face for Ranvir, who would be waiting to pick her up at the airport in Chennai.

3

"Aaradhya! Aaradhya! come in baby. It's already past seven. You have a lot of homework to finish. Enough of play now!" yelled Ayesha over the boundary wall across the street where Aaradhya, her ten year old daughter was playing with her friends. Aaradhya paid no heed to the first call, as usual.

Ayesha looked desolate, true to her floating life as a single mother circumstantially forced to be so. Yash had bid her goodbye one day into her fourth year of blissful marriage, to try his luck in a far off dreamland called USA. She had been enthralled then. The thought of spending a peaceful life in luxury was panacea to her pangs of forced separation for the initial period of her getting a visa to join her husband. Yash had been a software engineer and with the ever growing demand of Indian talent abroad was increasingly impatient to cross the waters. The moment he got the opportunity, he jumped at it without blinking an eyelid for a thought as to who would take care of his pregnant wife, especially when they already had the stigma of an inter-religious, love marriage so despised by his own family. Ayesha had no one to turn to. For she was the sole survivor of her father who had settled for a second wife after Ayesha's mother had died of cancer when she was just eleven. Her stepmother never made bones about her despicable disposition being unable to produce her own progeny. Yet she made good by throwing Ayesha out, when Sardar Khan died by usurping all that Ayesha's father had left on his death bed. Ayesha had just turned eighteen then.

"Aaradhya! Enough of it now!" she yelled harshly enough to bring her running in, panting to catch her breath. "Sorry Mamma", she replied innocently. Her face flushed from all the running. Ayesha could hardly swallow the lump that was fast forming in her throat. "Baby, please be serious about your studies now. Exam's just round the corner now!" she chided. Then as she watched Aaradhya slip slowly into her desk to complete her homework, Ayesha drifted back into her own thoughts. "Oh Yash!" she sighed.

After being thrown out, Ayesha had shifted to an old dilapidated house that once belonged to her dead mother. One that Sardar Khan had been wise enough to register in Ayesha's name in a belief to dispose it off in future for marrying her off comfortably. There are times when the trial by the Almighty is a never ending process for some. And Ayesha lived to testify this. Into her twentieth year, she had paid off her graduation by selling homemade chocolates and toffees, an art she had learnt while observing her father at work in his confectionery shop, as a teenager. The money was barely sufficient to make both ends meet, but enough to sustain life without much glitch. Adversity teaches one to become self reliant. Ayesha saved the pennies to get her house repaired and was soon able to let out a portion of her old house for rent. Fortunately for her the locality was good and there was a steady flow of tenants to supplement her modest income from confectionery.

Yash floated back in her thoughts. It had been a rainy day. Ayesha had gone to deliver chocolates to a neighbor for their child's birthday party. Her chocolates were sought as novelty and a tasty return gift for remembrance. In her hurry to avoid getting drenched, she had dashed into the party house, only to bang into a handsome hunk, Yash. It was a wonderful coincidence, for Yash, the youngest son of the family had just returned from his studies as a software engineer and in his eagerness to prevent the splashing rain wetting, the alleyway, had rushed to close the door. Before he could shut the door the door swung open and caught him off balance for time enough to collide with someone extremely beautiful. A scene yanked off from a romantic film. Seconds of silence, the wet clothes and the instinctive clinging for support that both had to do when they lurched, had landed them into each other's arms. Both recovered quickly, apologetic yet amused. That first collision was to have a long lasting impact. Both were attracted to each other and were soon eagerly waiting for each other's company in cozy corners of cafés around the town. Yash had by that time joined a local software company and was more mobile to take Aayesha out more often. Young love of the two twenty's something flowered and one day Yash proposed to Ayesha, who was at once elated and sad. Elated because it was perhaps the only good thing to have happened in her drab life since her mother died. Sad, for she was a Muslim and Yash, a Hindu. "Your parents will never accept me", she told Yash. But, Yash would have none of it. And, so it was after a fiercely contested battle of words with his parents that Yash left them to marry Ayesha in the Courts. He had shifted to Ayesha's old house and both were blissfully wedded till the economy started overshadowing matrimony in their life. Yash was ambitious. He was qualified but grossly underpaid for his knowledge. USA had been in his dreams since childhood and with passing time had become his passion. He applied online for many companies and one fine morning got his dream offer. He was on cloud nine. Ayesha had shyly confided her pregnancy to him just a day before. "Oh! You are so lucky", he lovingly patted his wife's tummy for fondly communicating to his future offspring. Ayesha was dumbfounded. She found it hard to reconcile the joy of a new life that was taking shape in her own body with the fact that the cause of that joy would now no longer be there to help her through the trials of motherhood. "Oh God! Seems like my joys are limited", she sobbed silently, her pale smile camouflaging the tears that welled in her eyes. The pain of loneliness is dreadful and no one could know it better than her. Her tribulations had just begun again, perhaps with a vengeance.

"Mamma!Mamma, How many states are there in the USA?" Aaradhya nudged her, bringing her back from the alleys of past to the present courtyards. "Umm! 51", she replied, drifting back into another swirl of never ending thought streams. Aaradhya was born exactly eight months after Yash had left for USA. It had been an extremely difficult phase for her. It was indeed fate that had sent a small family as her tenants who helped her through the ordeal. They had in fact become the God parents of young Aaradhya. Two years later, Ayesha had boarded a flight to the US to meet Yash in a firm belief to reunite and settle down. Yash had sent her a return ticket though citing a limitation of tourist visa then. "We shall work something out, don't worry" he had cajoled holding young Aaradhya fondly. She had returned back after three months still confident of going back finally. "Oh! Its just a little too expensive here. Let me just build some reserve for a comfortable house first", Yash had called up in response to her e-mail expressing her solitude and yearning for reunion.

The damp replies soon petered out. Ayesha, though worried got herself busy in taking care of Aaradhya who remained the bonding that Yash still retained for communicating as and when he wanted.

Soon it was apparent that Yash had outgrown their once blissful relationship to move on to greener pastures abroad, not only for economic reasons but biological as well. She chanced to catch Yash in a conversation with Samantha, an office colleague once and now his live in US partner, while he was talking to young Aaradhya over the mobile which playfully she had kept on speaker mode. She now knew why the calls from US were infrequent and why there was always an economic reason for Yash not taking them there. Her world was shattered. She felt sick from inside and this soon reflected in her deteriorating asthma bouts coupled with the acute arthritic pain in her joints, a childhood illness that started revisiting her more frequently now. Her own defense of a strong intellect that had valiantly fought adversity till now suddenly started devouring herself. It was only Aaradhya that kept her waking up day after day.

Life changes with time. So do priorities. But the pain remains lingering. A woman alone can understand the ache of being pestered with adversities and yet being asked to sustain a smile. Motherhood brought her the resolve to dedicate her life towards making her daughter's life more secure—something that destiny had so brazenly denied her. Wiping off her tears, she wriggled out of the couch and slowly made her way to the kitchen for cooking dinner for her dear daughter, the only shining star in her dark nights of solitude.

Rental income supplement generated some reserve for her to delve into another business of providing a cab service attached to a local government office. A gift from her tenant who helped her, get the contract. As long as one of her father's old loyal driver could serve her, the venture proved to be beneficial. She was happy to afford a house and a car as well, something most well off persons cherish. Yet adversities were hand in glove with her destiny—gremlins they call it in technical parlance. With the transfer of the well wisher officer tenant, the new 'boss' of the establishment was uxorious enough to press the contracted vehicle to his wife's service. The bossy madam soon started nagging the driver, demanding even the car keys to be left in the evening to her custody. All this soon led to the harried driver quitting the service. Ayesha's car came to a standstill and with it the little extra income she managed. She had no choice but to sell of the car and trade off the income for a small vehicle for her personal use now that Aaradhya also needed to be taken to the ever growing pressure of tuitions and extra classes.

Moreover there was a break in her rental income also when the tenant left. But God has his own ways to mend and bend the flows of destiny. One day, Shrey came searching for a house in the locality that was near to his office where he had just been transferred. His local office contacts, good Samaritans they were, had brought him at the doorsteps of Ayesha. She had immediately taken a liking for Shrey who had a gentle but no nonsense disposition and who carried himself with grace. Shrey on the other had found the accommodation just apt for his forced bachelorhood in the sense that he was unable to shift Nitya and the children with him. The only problem was he was now single and so was the young and beautiful would be landlady who stood in the doorway showing him the first floor accommodation. "Nitya will never agree", he mulled over. "Madam", he politely addressed Ayesha, "Please give me three days to confirm back. Hope you can keep the house vacant till then. Rent is not a problem. I just need to talk it over with my family". Obviously Ayesha had agreed. That had been almost two years ago now.

Shrey had finally been able to cajole Nitya to allow him to accept Ayesha's place. In these two years, Nitya had had time for two extremely short visits. True to her gentle nature, she had soon found sympathy for Ayesha. Ayesha on the other hand also got comfortable with the presence of a responsible man in her own house whom she slowly started trusting. In fact for her and Aaradhya, there was a sense of security when Shrey was around because of the respect he commanded in society and who had in the months won admiration of the neighborhood for being able to create standards of decorum as a classy neighbor. Ayesha's respect grew even more when she discovered once day that Shrey's sister had once been her treating physician in another city and who had perhaps been the only doctor to have diagnosed her still continuing illness properly. It was another matter that she had to abandon the treatment when she had been forced to leave that city due to pressing circumstances created by her relatives with whom she had been putting up for treatment. They had upon knowing of Ayesha's condition for a long treatment started taking advantage of her for running household errands even as she had the burden of little Aaradhya in tow. Society is harsh for women and even harsher for single mothers. Therefore, Ayesha had been forced to return to her home, where now destiny had brought Shrey, her longest surviving tenant so far who had never ever complained about whatever she charged him for rent and the add-on services for arranging the housemaids, cleaning etc when he was out to office day after day. They had both worked out a practical system of keeping a spare set of Shrey's apartment keys for enabling her to manage the housekeeping, and it had worked well with each learning to trust the other for maintaining the clear boundaries of morality.

However, she would at times just find excuses to talk to the otherwise reserved Shrey. It could have been her own sense of insecurity, her own frustrations or simply a courtesy of sharing a conversation with immediate neighbor but it helped in forging a very different bonding between the two. There were times when she would sense some deviation in Shrey's otherwise methodical daily routine and immediately know something was wrong. She would then call up Nitya to ask if everything was all right, instead of approaching Shrey directly. Sometimes even this wall of diffidence she maintained out of respect as well as a distancing tool would be demolished to provide an ailing Shrey with food and arranging medicines. All such little measures made them open up for seeking and extending help to each other more often—once a very guarded move clouded in modesty.

Strange are the ways of God, who brings different persons together from all walks of life at on a common platform so much so that they start sharing their daily lives seamlessly even before a cognizance of the same dawns on them. Ayesha's relationship with Shrey stood as a testimony to this Divine intervention and in sharp contrast to the pedagogical prophesies of self proclaimed moral police in the society who view man-woman relations from a totally sexual inclination to start with. Acceptance of man and woman as independent human beings regardless of any sexual overtones perhaps, requires the society to mature from focusing on titillating teenage crushes to relationships groomed on trust—much beyond pure physical lusts, to being platonic. It is not that the sexuality is to be denied to the point of ascetic seclusion but to be considered as a normal existential fact that is as natural as breathing. The only difference is that sexuality cannot be the only overshadowing viewpoint of any man-woman relationship but just one of the many nuances that is present in varying degrees between two mature individuals.

4

Shaymolee, breezed through Shrey's cabin, "Hi. Just ask for some coffee for me".

No formalities, no misgivings. It was always like that. Shyamolee had been years junior to Shrey and had a chance of working in a same branch at Shrey's earlier place of posting. She however came to this town earlier than Shrey and was in another department of the same company. This however did not prevent both of them to share their mutual liking of the fine arts and literature.

Shyamolee was an accomplished stage artist and Shrey and Nitya would often be invited to her plays. "Wow! I just envy you both, Looks like you've just been made for each other. And look at your children. I just love to cite your example as the complete family", she would often state, whenever they were together in office or outside at parties. Shyamolee was therefore obviously delighted upon seeing Shrey again after a long gap.

"People here are so boring. Good that now you are here. We can again catch up on the literature and drama again", she continued even as Shrey ordered coffee and cookies for both of them. As administrative head of the branch office, he did have the privilege to get his coffee served in the cabin. He smiled, taking a break from his papers, "So, what's up"? "Aw! Nothing. But I just came up to ask you out for a new movie. I am not finding company and I can't go alone. Please don't say no. I've already got the tickets and I'm just informing you to be there by six in the evening today. C'mon, it's just Saturday and a weekend for everyone. Surely, you too can take a breather from extended working today. Please!" she continued in a monologue.

Shyamolee too had been a victim of forced bachelorhood like him. Her husband was working in another company and so could not accompany her to her new place of posting. They had no children, perhaps as a conscious decision. Now with the approaching middle ages the pinch of loneliness was clearly visible in her almost pleading tone for a company in this alien land. Shrey just shrugged, "Alright. I'll be there". No second thoughts there. Fifteen years his junior, Shyamolee always treated him like a friend. She was frank enough to discuss anything on this earth with him. The clarity of understanding between them was unsurpassed and did not have any sexual overtone at all. They had a truly platonic relationship. Both admired the other for their individual capabilities in the office and outside. Both had a common interest in reading books and would share them also along with critical commentaries. It was simple—both liked each other's company.

"Just be on time", said Shyamolee, gulping up the last sip of coffee and sailing through the cabin door almost simultaneously, dumping the paper coffee cup in the dustbin. Shrey went back to work. "At least today the evening would be enjoyable", he thought, "it's been months since I saw a movie. Nitya is always complaining and I could not take her out often. Let's see if this movie is worth going again with her next weekend when I go home".

Shyamolee arrived simultaneously in the parking lot with him and waved as she parked her car. Soon both were ushered in through the metal detectors to the lobby. There was still some time before the show started and Shrey bought some snacks and cold drinks to while away the time. He had not even bothered to ask her the movie's name or the star cast. So they waited and exchanged trivia while biting snacks before entering the hall. The show soon began and to utter surprise of Shrey, the double-entendre dialogues had him uneasy in a female company who certainly was not his wife. The film sailed through with some wit and humor thrown in. Once out he bid good-bye to Shyamolee and drove off to Ayesha's house, part of which he had rented out a year ago.

En-route he called up Nitya, as he would do every day and casually discussed his evening out with Shyamolee. At once he could sense some diffidence in Nitya's voice. It was not that she did not know Shyamolee or the fact that she was also posted in the same location as he was. It was something else. Perhaps the bitterness of being left alone to tender the family and his own freedom to spend time at will and that too with someone else had made her a bit reticent. For a moment she was quiet. And then suddenly the bund gave way to a flash flood of sobs and sighs—something that he had always dreaded. A man can lie to anyone but himself. In his heart of heart, he had felt the hesitation even as he had agreed to Shyamolee's offer in the morning. Was it guilt of leaving out Nitya? Had he cheated upon her? It was true that given the family circumstances, they had hardly been able to spend quality time with each other. So now if he had found time out with someone else, it was only natural that the sobs were a real hurt. He felt sorry for Nitya. She had been a dedicated and loving wife who had sacrificed her own love for classical dance just to take care of the family. She had been an accomplished dancer of eleven long years with some sterling stage performances to cherish. It was not that he was in a habit of enjoying such sojourns, but today had been different in a company he liked to be with. Perhaps this was a thorn that would prick Nitya for long. She complained, "It's OK. What else can I expect after so many years of marriage? I am just an old hag now. Isn't it"? Shrey was speechless—trapped in his own quagmire, too difficult to extricate. He needed space and that came in form of a traffic light. "Sweetheart, I'm sorry. I'll have to hang up. I'm at a traffic signal. Will call you later once I reach my place", he hurriedly hung up.

He quietly drove back home, ruminating the brief encounter with Nitya. He missed her, badly but there was nothing he could do. Life had taken such a twist that almost everything from job to parents to children had all apparently came up as blocks between him and Nitya. This was one relationship that was definitely not meant to be platonic. Yet it was more than a year that they both had started to feel the drift of aloofness that had surreptitiously crept in between their cozy relationship that had once been envy for all. Together they had shared a chemistry that is not generally visible in these times. It was trust and commitment that had provided a solid foundation of their married life with no room for anyone in between. Such was their faith in one another that nothing remained unshared between them. Truly they had understood the meaning of trust in building a relationship and the commitment that was required for developing that trust. So it was that today's sharing was like any routine exchange, but it had unintentionally created a wedge in their already spaced apart existence.

With a heavy heart, Shrey parked his car in the alley outside his rented abode and slowly opened the gate. Nitya's nagging complaint already had been pricking his conscience continuously. All in all, his Saturday evening was turning out to be too painful for nobody's fault. It was just circumstances that had juxtaposed a intermingling of competing thoughts coupled with the reactions of individual players on the scene as the drama had unfolded during the day. He silently cursed himself for something he had not done or had no intention to do—hurt his dear wife Nitya. Human relationships are such that these cannot be defined exactly. Nor can any psychology expert claim knowledge of being omniscient about them. They are purely individualistic and demand a commonsensical understanding by mature grownups in an objective manner. But it is precisely the subjectivity of an individual, emanating from being directly involved in the act that clouds the vision preventing him or her to empathize with the other person with whom the communication goes awry. So it had started happening between him and Nitya, and it was certainly sad. He longed to be with her for he respected her individuality more than anything—a sure sign of his unconditional love devoid of any collateral demand or expectations. But the circumstances that they had created by their own conscious decisions about their mutual roles in life were now actually proving to be constraints that restricted their hitherto free flowing life. One can compare the same with the turbulent flows of a river when it encounters rocky beds to those in the plains—the water is the same only the contours shape the flows.

It was late already and the thought of cooking dinner was agonizingly irritating him. With the muddle of thoughts he slowly started climbing the stairs when suddenly Ayesha called him from behind. She was holding a plate. "You are late today. Here's something I had tried tonight. I made some for you too. So no need to cook tonight", she smiled, as if reading his mind. "Thanks", he said as he gratefully he accepted the plate and smiled back. "Aaradhya's asleep?" he asked. "Actually I had something for her", he fished out chocolates from his pocket and thrust into Aayesha's hand, as if it were a return gift in gratitude. Aayesha looked for a while in his eyes as if silently asking what was wrong. Then nodding her head in acknowledgement of confirming Aradhya having slept, turned and went inside carrying the chocolates.

5

It had been two weeks since Kaavya had returned from her meeting and a wonderful refreshing meeting with Ranvir at Chennai.

Trial came sooner. Shrey chanced to text her, a message congratulating her for her forthcoming interview for an MBA degree in a prestigious institute of international repute, that too abroad. He had in a lighter vain commented that perhaps this was just one of his few odd messages left for whatever time she would be working in the organization now. For her it was however a trigger that led to an emotional disclosure of her feelings in front of him. He was astounded. She left him tearful and visibly disturbed—something she had not seen before. He had not called up or sent any daily customary educative messages for days thereafter. Aloofness that had crept in his demeanor suddenly appeared cold to her. She would also surreptitiously turn her back to him at times, as if returning something in kind, while sharing space in a corridor.

Then one day he walked into her cabin, something he had done after many days. He pulled a chair and sat down. "You appear serious. What's the matter?" he had asked her. "Why do you ask? It's you who has made me serious. Isn't it?" she had coldly retorted. A pained look in his watery eyes crossed for a while. "Look, I cannot spoil lives! especially yours. You know it as well. But I still want to apologize for having intruded into your life unintentionally. You need to understand that this relationship can never be more than anything platonic, nothing beyond unconditional friendship", he had said, as he walked out bowing in courtesy.

He might have put up a brave face in front of Kaavya, but his own conscience nagged him now. He recalled how Nitya had once sagaciously told him to maintain distance from Kaavya. "Look, I am a woman. And I know what goes on in a female mind. She is so young and inexperienced in the ways of the world. Be careful as there could be some misunderstanding of gestures. I trust you with your wisdom and clarity but I cannot vouch the same for someone else. Honey, things can become complicated. Control yourself! Avoid those freelance communications of yours! Please", she had pleaded. He had just laughed it away, "C'mon. They are all sensible educated professional young adults, half my age. They have perhaps better definitions than us to think on a more emotional plane". Nitya had never agreed and today she had just been proved right. He had virtually been caught off guard and this had created an imbalance which he found difficult to accept. He just could not understand that someone half his age could still find him attractive for expressing love—puppy love he called it. "How can she do it? It's insane? Why is she bent upon spoiling her life with such thoughts? She knows what my family means to me. She knows Nitya. She Knows what Nitya means to me?" he had just bombarded himself with pondering questions that he could never answer himself. These were serious questions though seemingly simple. But more than that, the trouble was how to share this emotional sub-atomic explosion with Nitya. "God how am I going to face her?" he was worried.

It was not that he was getting swayed simply by a beautiful young woman half his age who had just confessed her own feelings for him. Instead it was the pain that his belief in someone he had considered to be sensibly different than most had been shattered. He was at a loss to understand that the special relationship he had so fondly nurtured being an out of the world experience was petering down to the mundane sexuality angle. But his deep seated respect for Kaavya, his admiration for her skills as an excellent officer, her inherent qualities as a person were now at crossroads with her emotions.

It has now been days since she had talked to him on professional matters even. He had still tried to maintain the ethics alive with routine mails and messages but there never was a response. On top of it her questioning eyes, if ever they met his briefly during the 'good morning' nods or in the corridor were full of sadness that pricked him for being a culprit without having committed any crime. He had never foreseen that that a relationship he had so carefully cultivated would end up so harshly. The pain was overwhelming and it was made worse by the fact that he had to endure it alone—without even his dear Nitya to support.

In his two years of separation from Nitya, never had he felt lonely as now. He had managed his life through all turmoil with a belief that now he had an extended family to care for. He felt secluded and this depressed him. Loneliness was already a curse that he had endured since his transfer here. It was now that having lost the one relationship he considered as the kindling light in an otherwise dark night had actually sounded a death knell of sorts to his emotions.

Nitya sensed this fast and during her daily telephone calls could make out his discomfort from his edgy comments and short answers. This is what trust and commitment does in relationship. When two people are committed to each other they do not need senses to verify their actions. Their minds probably read each other without any spoken exchange. Yet she wanted him to open up and express his own bottled up emotions so that the stress could be released. However, like most human beings, she correlated his discomfort arising out of her own reactions to both his anniversary gift and the outburst she had on his lone sojourn to a movie with Shyamolee. "Perhaps I've been too selfishly possessive about him. But I just can't help feeling so. I just can't share him with anyone", she had lamented to herself one day.

6

Life trudged on with each character burdened by own imaginary thoughts. Human beings are at times the most unreasonable of creatures because of their gift of thought—the very special gift from God that has made them masters of this planet. Their own reactions to their own actions are so jumbled that they lose the focus. Some things that can just be talked out calmly to avoid commotions and bickering, stealth and avoidance are simply dreaded. This is what leads to breach of trust amongst closely bonded individuals who end up developing unfathomable cracks in their otherwise solid relationships.

Shrey, Kaavya, Nitya—for all their self proclaimed wisdom were prisoners of this very fallacy they harbored so cherishingly within themselves. They just could not accept the fact that it was nothing but pure unconditional love that had bonded them in the first place. It was only when the lust element overpowered their initial affinity, that their vision became clouded by their own perceptions.

Kaavya, being the youngest and without any strings of commitment attached was perhaps in the easiest of the situation to have boldly blurted out her feelings for Shrey, notwithstanding either the consequences or the fact that this was a mirage, never to have a happy ending either way it worked. Nitya on the other hand had too much at stake, now that her own life was tied to so many commitments that her own individual self had been submerged forever in a fathomless ocean of emotions. Shrey was the worst of all as he had everything to lose—friendship, face, faith, trust and love, all at the same time from whichever side he chose to walk out. But perhaps neither Kaavya nor Nitya had either the inclination or the intention of understanding his position.

From the moment Kaavya had made her feelings known to Shrey, he had not been a normal person. Who would be? Nitya had sensed something from his dry monosyllable responses and bouts of depressing talks. One day she just confronted him by asking about Kaavya's well being. Shrey was expecting this and quickly explained that the busy work schedules had all but made their interactions brief and infrequent. Nitya overtly acknowledged the fact in an understanding manner but was woman enough to keep the instinctive antennae alert for any alarm signals. She would therefore, now and then drive back to her focused subject for eliciting more viable information that could satisfy her. Shrey would not budge. He had already lost one front for no fault of his and was aware that any loose statement could be interpreted in any way that could damage his position on home front as well. He cursed himself silently in his solitude nights for being naïve enough to befriend a female half his age and these thoughts had now started gnawing at his conscience. Another great folly as he was now playing to his emotions with focus on Kaavya. The Puritanical had drifted into wishful thinking—lust was now less than Platonic. It was now more human. The stress began to tell on his health and it reflected in long bouts of illness and careless little accidents where the pain was more pronounced due to apathy of someone who had cared for him not so long ago. The expectations were back in the game and this time he was at the receiving end. Alone and away from his own beloved Nitya, the sheer ignore from Kaavya unsettled him

He tried to work his way out by attempting to breach the divide by directly talking to Kaavya. But her rebuttals were fierce and extremely painful to the point of scathing attacks. Was it that she too had sensed the folly in her own attempts and was now trying to stifle her emotions by putting up a hard face? Was it that she was really angry at being rebuffed by a male old enough to be an uncle who she had preferred over the marauding studs that made a perfect match of youth and energy with her beauty? Was it revenge that she now sought in inflicting pain on someone she just passionately loved till a few days ago? Shrey had thought these over and over being a gentleman to respect the modesty of a young beautiful female. Yet he could find no answer. This troubled him as it became a battle of nerves for him clearly affecting the routine office work. He suddenly found himself lonely and up against wall facing an adversary he had neither the intention nor the will to fight. He pondered how Bhishma Pitamah in the epic Mahabahrata must have felt before Shikhandi.

Times just change without warning. And this change is more apparent when troubles are round the corner. Shrey was in a similar quandary. Maintaining a professional etiquette in front of a hostile adversary who is hell bent on aggressive response is extremely difficult. Kaavya had made her intentions very clear. It was either a strictly professional relationship or a personal one and it had to be Shrey's call. "Women! They are so difficult to understand!" Shrey fumed. He could do little but abide time to normalize situations. So he turned inwards and started maintaining a stoic silence while dealing with his now indifferent subordinate, someone he still respected from the core of his heart.

It needs no Freudian insight to understand that when egos play ball, the relationships take a toll. So it was with the three of them. Each with his or her, own mindset had knitted a cobweb of sorts that contained their own emotions in a manner that they became painfully obvious to the other. They were all so engrossed in analyzing the other from their own "my perspective" that a mountain was growing out of a mole. Was there a way out? So much for the platonic aspects of man—woman relations.

Time is the biggest healer of all. Nothing escapes time and so it was that the coldness between Kaavya and Shrey had to end. The wise always say "this too shall pass", and so the coldness between them had to go. As it was, their work was unnecessarily suffering and becoming obvious to others. So, one morning, finding Kaavya a little free and alone in her cabin, Shrey walked up and calmly sat down in the visitor chair opposite her desk. Minutes passed. None spoke. The heat of silence ultimately melted the cold ice wall that had crept between them. Shrey, being the elder was the first to let go of his ego. "I am sorry for having hurt you. But believe me, there was no intention of either being harsh or cut up on any issues with you. I respect you so much that I can never even think of causing pain to you. Still if inadvertently I did cause you the pain, I can only seek one more chance. Let's be friends again." That was it. Kaavya was perhaps herself waiting for this catharsis. With tears welling in her eyes she looked up and said, "Sometimes your actions do not match your words. It is really difficult to understand you". Shrey was taken a little aback but he said with poise "Come on. Let bygones be bygones. We both know the reality of our relationship and also know of our individual commitments to the ones we love and care. I think this is a very good learning for both of us to mature our relationship to a higher level of understanding. Can we not really start a fresh page with higher confidence in each other?" Kaavya nodded and smiled. Time is indeed the biggest healer.

7

Were life as simple as a math equation, it would have left everyone happy with a solved problem and a content mind for having reached an acceptable conclusion. This however is not what life actually is. Complexity arises from this "mind" and its thought processes. No two individuals can think alike and rightfully so because their intellect perceives any signal differently enough to analyze in a distinctive manner. It is only a working consensus in real life situations that determines the outcome of any event—good or bad, depending upon whose logic prevails or who is more pliable for a resolution.

Shrey and Kaavya had buried the hatchet and resumed their dialogue is a more mature way. There was now a greater sense of enjoyment in each other's company. It was a marvel that sans the lust their relationship had actually transcended on a much higher level with a more spiritual tilt than mere physical attraction of being close. This new mingling of minds and the thoughts, candid sharing of views without any chords attached had opened up new levels of communication hitherto unknown. Their relationship was now actually assuming platonic proportions.

One day out of sheer boredom of living alone and missing his family, Shrey decided to go out for lunch. Just as he thought about it, Kaavya had ventured into his cabin for some official work. Unplanned as it was, he just asked her if she was free to accompany him for lunch. Kaavya too just accepted the invite on its face value. So both just went out and spent the lunch time together. It was that simple, but complexities arise without warning and so when Nitya's phone rang right in the middle of a morsel, Shrey told her that he would call her back shortly for he did not feel to discuss anything personal in front of Kaavya and also from the fact that Nitya would react differently if she came to know who his lunch partner of the day was.

One can compare relationship akin to a building. Understanding is the foundation stone on which any love relationship is based. Trust is the cement that bonds the bricks of togetherness. Therefore, any breach of trust, even if perceived by one of the partners in a love relationship, can actually weaken the bond. If one compares the impact of forced separation, responsibilities, avoidance due to social pressures or simply taking a relationship for granted to some external forces that affect a building over time, the similarity can actually be visualized in terms of the cracks that become visible in relationships. No one is exclusively at fault, but collectively adds on to the decay.

The small episode of Shrey's lunch with Kaavya was enough to bring Nitya at her furious best. It was painful for both of them but in a different manner. For her it was perhaps an expression of unknown, inexplicable frustrated fears that had gripped her in a sense of losing out to a young competitor. For him it was simply a case of another misunderstanding. But for each the spat left a bad taste. There were obvious reconciliatory moves like one often sees between border disputes of India and China, but the coldness was dampening the fires that they had so lovingly kindled over their twenty years of marriage.

Shrey suddenly found himself suffocated. All his logic, reasoning and efforts for keeping his exchanges with Kaavya transparent and free from the mundane clutter had no effect on Nitya. It was indeed sad as there had been no deliberate intentions on his part to foster any extra marital relationship. His relationship with Kaavya had been purely platonic so far and both were committed to it as each knew about the other's commitment to their individual soul mates. But as a true soul mate he sat thinking from Nitya's point of view. It became apparent that his reaction is such situations would not have been much different. Nitya's fears were certainly not unfounded, given his own admissions of interactions with Kaavya, no matter how innocent or asexual. His Platonic Lusts were certainly not free of the bond he had come to share with Kaavya, something which Nitya found transgressing her own rightful territory.

The story goes on with each character playing the role that circumstances have created, but it is clear that a stable platonic relationship between a man and woman whether narrated through Kaavya and Shrey or Aayesha and Shrey or Shyamolee and Shrey is possible if one opts for it rather than falling in for the purely opportunistic lusts for which each of the characters in the story had ample latitude and opportunity in a very conducive environment that had essentially brought them close. But Shrey now has an additional onerous task to start again on re-building the trust in Nitya's mind, something that had taken a dent, though inadvertently by the very environment that had helped him forge new platonic relationships without involving her.

NIGHT ON A TRAIN

---------------- ✛ ----------------

The Engine whistled brazenly and the train started slipping across the station. The conundrum increased in the bogie. People who had been loitering around, peering through the windows suddenly became active and dashed to aboard.

The second class sleeper coach, in which I had managed to get a *tatkal* ticket was fast filling up with people—with reservations, without reservations, expectant travelers, accompanying travelers of expectant travelers, routine friends of the daily up-down crowd etc. Soon the coach was filled way past its capacity with a curious grazing of standing and sitting bodies of different shapes sizes and sex, twitching noses and besmirched faces. Laughter and anguish co-exited with equanimity but with a complementary role when seen from either the unintentional offender or the purposely offended point of view.

Train journeys have always enticed me—each with a new experience, each in a different company. True to the fact this one was also with its own flavor.

The journey was a short one of five hours and as my destination was scheduled a half past midnight in cold December, I had to work out ways to keep myself from falling asleep and the people around offered me the very opportunity to do so. I even found interesting names to describe the co-passengers for ease of connection.

Gupta ji and his wife both occupied the lower berths in the coupe. Both wore thick lenses, probably with age or post cataract operations. Their unkempt clothes and the sparse luggage both indicated a tired life with weariness of a long wait for that elusive happiness that most of us try to find by looking at others. No sooner had the train started lady Gupta ji found enough space to cuddle up on the berth for an eventual stretch out. Her years of toil, perhaps gave sufficient practice to comfortably lie on the cold, hard berth without the luxury of any sheet to cover. Folded hands under the head were the best pillow provided by nature to make her oblivious of either the clickety-click of train wheels or the noisy cabin or the chilly wind that intruded through the loose shutters on the windows. Gupta ji continued to focus on the crushed newspaper much beyond.

Trains are the common man's connection with reality—the urbanization of rural small towns. The group of four—three, seated next to Gupta ji, and one at the edge of my side berth—as it turned out were the daily up-downers to the City from their small town located two hours away. So it was convenient that the trains travelling to and fro in the morning and evening offered the best means of connectivity—even at the cost of someone else's inconvenience who was a co-passenger. Whatever one may say, reservations of seat offer a consolation of conditional occupancy to the traveler with forced sharing of such luxury with the daily intruders who perhaps even the ticket collectors have now got used to.

Next to lady Gupta was a duo, who were the eventual occupants of the upper berths. Fashionably dressed in track suits, sports shoes, knapsacks and of course the headphone connects to the ubiquitous mobile phones, they appeared to be heading home for the weekend. Quiet observers, both soon found comfort in stretching across on the upper berths.

The train gathered speed. It was full of people still struggling to settle down. I visualized a large box of large and small stones, which when shaken ultimately settled in the spaces available, leaving some stragglers searching in vain the comfort of the sleeper berth on an ordinary ticket. Surely vestibule trains have their advantages—you can move end to end for half the journey and the other half will pass in company of similar less endowed co-passengers. Maulana was one of them. Young, sturdy with a flowing beard reflecting a person who had already tasted the blessings of Haj. Accompanied by Ahmed, perhaps his cousin, from appearance, both were anxiously looking down the alley for locating a suitable place to sit which however was not there. Time passed, and they settled down to share bread and condiments near the door itself. After all hunger and sleep are such overpowering urges that ultimately command even in the surroundings deprived of hygiene. They were soon joined by another duo from the next bogie and thereafter the banter of exchange in this group was louder than the rickety coach noise. They had perhaps found ways to overcome the unavailable.

My thoughts were interrupted by a gentle nudge on my shoulder. It was who I recalled as a lookalike of one Hariram uncle. Dressed in a beige safari, gold watch and good shoes, he appeared to be a diabetic with a frequent urge to ease himself in the toilet. During the journey this to and fro movement by Hariramji was standard clockwork, He was awake and so were many others.

Down the alley I noticed Dolly with her doll like baby, incessantly crying. What could it be? Hunger? Stomach ache? Cold? Or the Inability to sleep amongst the conundrum? I was taken back to my own children in similar situation. I tried to recall what my dear wife had done then to tackle the trouble. Even as I mentally retraced the cause to a wet diaper, Dolly soon realized this and put her baby to comfort, who, then dozed off blissfully. Hariram ji had made another move.

I was again brought to the present by a request—"Bhaisaheb! may I share the seat with you?" I looked up to see an eager face expecting a positive response. He soon got one and in seconds was seated between me and fourth member of the four up-downers.

The diminutive ticket collector soon appeared, trailed by an armed guard and of course a milieu of eager followers expecting a berth from nowhere. Boy! people have guts to board the train without reservation and then spend time travelling across with luggage crushing other seated co-passengers with such élan as if they owned the train. One such Lord of the Train crushed by foot without even a second thought of apology. On the other hand reality also struck me that I too had obtained a fortunate *tatkaal* reservation under emergency. Surely the strugglers must be facing similar situation and they perhaps had no choice but to explore possibilities. This is India!

The monotone of ticket chart rummaging over, the cloud of commotion soon vaporized to descend on another bogie, taking along the newcomer on my berth. The up-downer as it turned out during the ticket checking was part of group of railway employees and hence was better endowed in terms of forced occupancy rights. Anyway, minutes later the train chugged to halt and the up-downers got down. Stoppage was for a couple of minutes and passengers many. There were ladies howling to get down even as equal number pushed them back to get in. I fail to understand why the basic discipline of entry and exit is amiss in such a situation where struggle benefits no one and could perhaps lead to an accident even. The railway staff, as usual were indifferent as all passengers sans humility.

A new set of expectant passengers had boarded including the stereotypes of Sharma family next door. Middle aged in a old discolored suit, Sharma ji was accompanied by his squabbling wife and two grown up daughters. Gathered next to Maulana even as train re-started, they made expectant searches for finding space which apparently was a scarce commodity. Expectations make a person take all chances, even when the probability of returns is extremely low in case of single persons, what to say of a whole family! Undeterred Sharmaji and family fluttered across bogies to eventually come back to the boarding spot and while away time in the night, standing.

Interspersed in the above unfolding of drama, were the omnipresent tea and snack vendors. Tea is a widely respected beverage across the sub-continent and it was so in the bogie as well. Jeetu, the tea vendor with his nasal call of "Chai!Chai", a tap container in one hand and paper cups stacked up in a cover in the other trudged up and down the alley. He would on call put the kettle down and place a paper cup under the tap, on the floor, to fill three quarters for five rupees. When I had boarded the train, I had noticed with distaste that the water from the toilets washing in the yard had been left to spill across the alley and had made the floor messy with all the varied dirt and muck stuck to the shoes of tens of passengers moving across. The same floor was now a table top for filling in the paper cup, so happily being consumed by the very passengers who had walked over the soiled surface. Even as I could mull over the scene, Jeetu did another act par excellence. He put the glass stack squeezed between his legs near his crotch to take out currency change. Minutes ago I had seen him emerge from the toilet zipping up and picking up the can before descending in the coupe. I am also quite sure many other people had observed the same. But then I believe, the scales of hygiene are as varied as are the urges of the people—whether to sip tea in a train or to visit the toilet. I could see Hariramji get up for another visit.

It was nearing ten and the legal berth holders like me started stretching down, displacing the stragglers still keen on tasting forced hospitality. This was barring the next coupe which was occupied by a group of salesmen who were travelling back from the weekly field visits. They were exchanging notes, pulling down each others' legs and whiling away time for eventual get down. They were soon discussing which occupation was the best and where the money lay. The discussion was interrupted by a landlord farmer from a prominent agriculture belt who clearly stated that there was nothing better than agriculture from large holdings. No tax! Only appreciation! He was right. But then it was only for large holdings. Soon the discussion switched over to the benefits of MBA degree which with the mushrooming of numerous institutes offering diplomas instead had taken the zest out of it. It was an indeterminate discussion with no solution but only unanswered questions to which no one, perhaps ever listened what to say ponder and act for remedial action.

I stretched and tried to doze off, unable to eat the sandwiches I had hurriedly packed before leaving. But the frequent motion of Hariramji and the echoing banter of salesmen kept me awake long enough to close my eyes and pretend sleeping with on and off catching the eyes of expectant travelers still standing in the cold to obtain a seat, no matter what. Nothing could bring out the chasm between the haves and have-nots with more alacrity.

A CLOSE CALL

⚓

In many hospital corridors, I have often come across motivating slogans, boards and philosophic renderings. They touch, where they should. One of those that always moved me is the dialogue of a complaining soul with God who ultimately learns that during his times of trial, it was God who carried him as evident from his missing footprints on the sands of time he lived.

There are times when the unexpected happens. There are times when, such happenings are disastrous. There are times when some timely signals prevent disasters.

The event is still very clear in my memory. Twenty long years ago, I was working with a company in business of selling journals to institutes. Once such trip, related to a remotely located research institute for sheep and wool. In the vicinity of the institute, is a famous pilgrimage frequented by people on foot from far off. So when I told my parents about my tour plan, they asked if I could arrange for a vehicle for them to accompany to enable them to visit the pilgrimage while I attended to business.

Buses were infrequent and uncomfortable for aging parents. I had no vehicle but had a penchant for driving. So I sought help from a friend who had an old jeep which he happily lent.

We set off. The track was single and dilapidated. This was not bad considering that the traffic at that time was not much and at the same time the urbanization was still a far cry from today's juggernaut sprawl. Yet deceptions never fail to surprise. We had barely gone few kilometers that a crudely made speed breaker by the local villager, camouflaged under the shade of huge neem trees, appeared as if from nowhere. The old dilapidated vehicle had its limitations with both technology and luxury. The sudden braking action made it jump and swerve at the same time in a single motion even as we crossed the speed breaker. Everyone sitting had an unexpected shake and naturally had to attempt holding on to some prop before the eventual collision of some body part with the vehicle. My five year old niece, who had forcibly joined the group, fell off from the rear seat to the floor and bruised herself. As my mother and aunt busied themselves in attending to her head bump and bruises, others including my father tried to calm her down.

We started off again after a while. This was not a very auspicious of beginning, as one may say, especially when the child's parents were not around, but there was little one could do. There was work to be attended to and hence despite the commotion, we continued.

August is normally a monsoon month in this part of the country and naturally the surface run-offs take their toll on the road. That day was also no exception and coupled with the pot holes and hold ups by the large sheep herds on the road, the trip went on in a start and stop manner with frequent braking of the old dilapidated jeep.

Two uneventful hours later, the final destination appeared. I parked the vehicle and set off to work, leaving the group behind to enjoy their picnic under shade of neem trees that swayed gently in the afternoon August breeze.

Work done, in another couple of hours, I was now ready to be at disposal of the family for their visit to the pilgrimage nearby and so we set out again through the village slush and accumulated rainwater. The trip to the temple was uneventful and the family was happy in having at last accomplished what they had set out to do.

Offerings over, it was time to start back to be home before dark. So the old jeep was on its way back home. Somehow return journeys seem that they are always short. Perhaps I had thought of it too soon!

We had barely gone fifteen kilometers that suddenly a stray goat scampered from the fields. I had to brake—but the pedal just went down and down with no stopping. I swerved and saved the goat. Then swiftly changing gears I brought the vehicle to a roll which then eventually stopped on the empty road—something to be thanked for at that time. I got down ascertaining what had happened. I observed oil leakage near the drum on the driver side and in a moment it was clear. There was no fluid left to make the hydraulics work for breaking the motion. It must have been the morning brake and jump over the speed-breaker that had caused the old lines to be under pressure which eventually burst and leaked the oil—something which went un-noticed till now. We were practically stranded with India still ages away from the cult of the mobile for connecting with civilization. Not a soul in sight and nearest township another fifteen kilometers away, it was a difficult situation with family and a young child of five in tow.

I mulled over the choices and having found only one decided to continue slowly till we reached the nearest town and located a mechanic for whatever repairs we could get. Fortunately this was aided by a half empty brake oil pack lying at the back in the jeep which I immediately used to part-fill the container for pumping whatever little aid I could get en-route. It was risky, with the bad roads and all the previous experiences with goats and speed breakers during the day.

The journey seemed eternal and as if on trial, we soon had vehicles coming across from front and behind. I had little choice but to cut back to rolling and let them pass. In an hour or so we somehow managed to reach the nearest town. The real test was about to begin now. With people on the village roads and traffic on the move, our jeep without breaks could cause havoc even with a minor scrape. Another problem was how to stop the vehicle in the town with little rolling space and more so where to find the mechanic. Everyone was praying in own style.

Prayers were answered and soon I saw a mound of sand near a wall which provided a perfect barrier, to bring the jeep to a halt, which it ultimately did. Leaving the family with the vehicle, I located a mechanic near the village bus stand. He was busy by the village standards and had to be lured for attending the jeep on priority leaving his regular customers in waiting. He asked me to bring the jeep to his shop and with great apprehension I finally managed to park the vehicle using the inclined slope between the road and the shop. He identified the problem, already known to me after examination and was candid in informing that the repairs could only be done in the city. However, he could temporarily fix up the leakage and this would mean that the breaking action will have to be carefully done with multiple pumping of the pedal to build pressure. This meant that there would be eventual loss of brake fluid under pressure. Did I have a choice? I just got the hint and with the repairs done and fill up of brake fluid, I sought another can of brake fluid for using as top up on the way to have enough liquid for a continued breaking action. The trouble would actually start in the outskirts of city with traffic and frequent breaking action required.

Slowly, the seemingly longest forty kilometer journey to home was made, with each kilometer covered easing the nail biting tension equivalent to the Indian Cricket team chasing forty runs in four overs! The outskirts of city appeared on the horizon along with the variety of traffic. We had managed the most and now the crucial city traffic had to be circumvented for a safe return.

Past sundown and many anxious moments, we finally made home without anymore events. I thanked God and retraced the events to see His footprints on the sands of time where my jeep tyre-marks faded into nothingness of a very close call.

VISION BEYOND A VIEW

✟

Children had all gathered around grandmother. It was the best time each night. Grandma would share her tales handed down from generations—stories that had significant learning stored in their simple messages.

Anil being the youngest always occupied the best place amongst all his siblings—his grandmother's lap. He adored her. She had a never ending collection of tales that she related each day. But for the much older children, who had grown to understand a little better, it was the message that grandmother subtly conveyed each day. It was a wonderful education of real life practical experiences that they got which perhaps no book or teacher could provide anywhere to anyone.

"Grandma, Grandma! What's the message today", all started in chorus, settling down grandma as she slowly got up and tried to recline against the wall. Anil as usual was quick to snuggle up in her lap with his little arms garlanding her neck. She hugged him and cleared her throat. "Today let us learn about observation", she said. "What's that?" asked Shyama, Anil's eldest sister in her early teens. "Well observation means to see but it is different than merely looking", grandma calmly required, expecting a barrage of the usual questions—how, why, what does it mean etc. "What is the difference between looking and observation then, grandma?" they all started again together. "Well for one observation is looking keenly with understanding what is happening. One becomes a part of the happening and relates to the actual event. Looking is merely being a spectator with no involvement in the event. You actually need to develop a vision beyond a view", she said. "No, grandma, it is too difficult. How can one look and yet not understand?" Shyama evinced more interest being a little sensible. "You see if one simply looks at anything without comprehending the significance in relation to the environment, one misses out the lesson. But observation is actually experiencing the happening oneself—and the learning remains forever etched on our minds. To clear the difference, here listen to today's story of Ramu, the young shepherd", grandma replied, as the children nestled close to her with keen interest, to learn something new. They just loved grandmother for her valuable tips she so lovingly shared with them. So grandma started narrating the story of a young shepherd boy, Ramu who made his living by tending the village goats.

One summer day, the sun was high up and the heat searing. Ramu had long gone to the grazing grounds with the goats since morning and the village elders had settled at the village Chaupal, when suddenly there was a conundrum of beating hooves and dust filling up the lane. "Hush! Hush!

It'll rain soon. Come let's reach shelter before then", Ramu the shepherd boy, repeated aloud, even as he crossed the village square. He rushed along as his herd made its way through the dusty lanes. He was soon away from the sight of the elders sitting on the village *chaupal* gossiping and sharing the hookah. Looking up at the blue sky through the swaying Neem leaves, that cast shadow over the *chaupal*, Gora the *Sarpanch* muttered, "The boy seems to have lost his head in the heat. It's a full bright day with Sun beating down fire on our heads". Bhura, his hookah partner was even sarcastic, "It's today's generation. Just doesn't want to work. Did you not see him run? I'm sure he wants to go out and fool around". With the grumbles and mutters the others nodded head in unison and went back to their gossip groups and hookahs.

The sky was clear and bright indeed. The weather was hot with little wind blowing. The boy was soon forgotten and soon the elders retired on the floor under the tree shade for their afternoon siesta, their usual pastime of the day. Hardly had some time lapsed that they were rudely woken up by the trickling drops of water on their bodies. All woke up with a start to find a dark cloud above with raindrops falling. It rained a while as a downpour and then as if the cloud satisfied with its deed drifted away to let the bright sun soak everyone in its light again.

All were aghast. Gora was the first to come out of the stupor. "Quick someone locate the shepherd boy. Must be in the rocky shelter at the foothills", he rasped and then gestured to two of the younger men in the direction the shepherd had gone. Sometime later, the two villagers returned with shepherd Ramu in tow carrying a small goat-kid in his arms. He looked perplexed at being summoned to the village *chaupal*.

Gora looked up and gestured him to sit next to him. Ramu was even more confused. "Surely these people are going to beat me. Must be something wrong I have done," he shivered silently awaiting some punishment to be pronounced. He had heard from his widowed mother the harsh penalties that the elders would often levy on the poor and downtrodden. "Must be that I have disturbed them by rushing through this way, earlier in the day", he thought and sighed. He meekly sat on the steps of the *chaupal*, just below where Gora sat. Gora looked at him hard, "What black magic is this? How did you make this rain happen? Tell me boy!" rasped Gora. His stout presence and a hoarse voice itself led credence to the stories about his high handed attitude in dealing with the lowly villagers. Ramu was really scared. No words came out of his mouth. He simply sat with downcast eyes stroking the goat-kid gently. "Tell me. What is this witch craft?" thundered Gora.

Trembling and afraid, Ramu barely able to control his sobs looked up slowly, "Sir, I do not know of any witch craft. I am a poor shepherd. I did not make the rain happen. Why are you angry with me? What wrong have I done? I just ran to protect your goats only", he blabbered. Gora calmed down and soothed him gently, "Son, don't be afraid. We old men are little amazed. It is a sunny day. Yet you ran taking the goats to shelter from rain. We all laughed and thought you were going mad in the heat. But we were all so wrong. It really rained. Tell me how did you know in advance? Are you a seer? On hearing this Ramu was relieved. He looked around at anxious eyes that stared him back, cleared his throat and spoke, "Sir, it is no miracle. I was grazing the goats like I do daily. It was hot and I sat under a shady tree. The goats grazed out in the sun and some sat around me in the shade. Suddenly, I saw a large snake come out of a pit across the ground and hurriedly climb a tree. Sir, I know from my herdsmen tales that small insects and reptiles have a better sense of the weather and they respond to warning signs much faster than we humans. In an open the snake would leave its pit only when it is afraid of being hunted or drowning. There was no one hunting for it. So it was natural for me to conclude that it would rain soon. Therefore I gathered the herd and took shelter. I am sorry if I offended your peaceful afternoon by rushing across from here. Please pardon me".

The elders were silent, perhaps ashamed of having mocked young Ramu. The lad was much wiser than themselves. He had learnt to keenly observe natural occurrence and take lessons. They had perhaps never grown up wise enough to see the simple signals that nature gave them. Gora looked at Bhura. Both had been sarcastic about the lad and his generation, yet it was Ramu's wisdom that had saved their herd from scattering away. Moreover, it was a lesson for each one to understand that the nature gave valuable signals all the time but most people failed to comprehend their significance due to their own assumed conditioned responses.

Grandma finished her story and looked at the now silent crowd of her young grandchildren who were in rapt attention still. They had learnt a valuable lesson on keen observation by a young lad that had realistic implications way beyond what met the eye. They now knew the difference between observation and simply looking at something. They had now experienced what having a vision beyond an ordinary view meant.

THE BOY NEXT DOOR

✟

"Coolie!Coolie", Shyamlata Nayak's shrill voice echoed in the early hours on the small railway station of Bilaspur. It was Six AM on a cold winter morning with few people around in the as yet "dark" morning. Sunrise was still a while away.

Like most people, the few coolies were also cozily snuggling on benches or large parcel packs. It was never a routine that someone would call them so early. "Perhaps another dream of a customer", Kishan yawned as he turned his back away from the train that has just arrived on the platform. "Coolie!Coolie", Shyamlata's shrill voice jarred his ears as he sneaked a peek out of his shawl through half shut eyes, trying to locate the source of the sound in the winter chill. Soon his focus froze on Shyamlata's white saree clad figure with three girls and a lot of baggage in tow. "Oh!Oh, seems like a party for a trolley," he jumped happily at the prospect of a good start for the day which otherwise was peaking at just over rupees fifty a day to keep the fires burning, both within and at home.

"Coolie, Madam", he said as he approached Shyamlata's who appeared graceful in her white saree. Then pointing to Shyamlata's luggage he said," That will be a hundred rupees—twenty five for the trolley and seventy five for the loading / unloading". He expected a negotiation and so had quoted a little higher. So he was surprised when a desolate looking Shyamlata quietly nodded in agreement. Her three daughters grouped around her as they all started following the trolley carrying their baggage, with Kishan whistling softly at his stroke of luck so early in the morning. For luck it was that he had Shyamlata as a good customer who was paying without fuss. He soon loaded the luggage on to a auto-tonga that Shyamlata had signaled, still whistling.

Had Kishan known Shyamlata's condition, perhaps his happiness would certainly have been dampened. Any other day also Shyamlata would not probably bothered to haggle on the coolie rates. Today was different. She was without Bindoo Babu, her husband. Tears welled in her eyes as she slipped back into her memories just two weeks back when all seemed so well in her life. Bindeshwari Dubey or Bindoo Babu as he was fondly referred by almost every one expired two weeks before. It had taken just minutes for him to bid her goodbye forever. "Shyama, get up I need some cold water with fruit salt, I have terrible acidity today", Bindoo babu has asked her that morning. She was not surprised knowing his habit of drinking whiskey every day followed by the usual bout of acidity. By the time she returned in less than five minutes with a bubbling glass of fruit salt, Bindoo Babu had gone. The glass fell and shattered on the ground as she unmindfully cut her naked feet with the shards, too numb to feel the blood or pain on seeing her world collapse. A true Indian Hindu housewife she had devoted her life in the confines of the rented houses in different cities that Bindoo Babu had taken her along in his service life. This time she had been a little happy as Bindoo Babu had been made a senior official in his company and provided a large bungalow with surrounding gardens, housekeeper and driver. It had seemed to her as a dream come true, something most middle class Indian women in her age in small towns had probably dreamt since their own college days. It was sheer ecstasy for her—dedicated husband, good living conditions, proper education for her three daughters, social status, what more could one ask for.

Alas! All seemed to have vanished in one small hiccup with which Bindoo Babu had breathed his last. Her dreams of settling her daughters lay shattered like the shards of glass that had cut her feet badly. The noise and her single shriek of terror had brought her eldest daughter Kamini running in. In a single moment the twenty five year science graduate had realized the catastrophe that had hit them all. Her father's corpse lay still in peace on the bed that had been his favorite place for years after dinner or on Sunday afternoons where he would simply lie inclined against bolsters and pillows with his newspapers or books—unmindful of his wife's constant reprimand on a never ending list of pending works. Her mother was now inconsolably weeping, gripping her dead husband's body tightly as if it would bring him back out of some slumber. Kamini stood aghast for minutes before walking up to her mother even as she shouted out to her younger siblings for help. As she approached her mother, her bare feet landed on something sticky in the dimly lit room. It was then that she saw that her mother was bleeding profusely with the soles of both her feet badly cut up though she was too unmindful of her own condition. "Ma!Ma", Kamini called out shaking her mother violently as if waking her up from the trance she was sinking into. Just then her younger sister Lata ran in and started wailing. "Shut up Lata", yelled Kamini "help me with Ma. She is hurt badly. Go get the first aid box from the cabinet in the toilet. Don't forget the Dettol!", she rasped. It was a real precarious situation and the normally shy Kamini found herself in a commanding position—hardly her choice though. There was work to be done—much work before she could even think of her own pain from the appalling tragedy that had unfolded before her like a typical Indian movie.

Soon, the news of Bindoo Babu's untimely demise had spread out to the neighborhood. With no relatives in the vicinity and the nearest ones three days away from his place of posting, it had been the office colleagues and subordinates who had done everything they could to help the four female survivors in Bindoo Babu's family from the funeral to the packing of their luggage for Bilaspur, Bindoo babu's old ancestral house, the only piece of property that he had possessed till his untimely death—the only place that Shyamlata had now turned back to.

Bindoo Babu had seen life every closely through his struggled existence in a middle class family and he knew the value of savings. He had been sagacious enough to utilize the prevalent insurance policies and post office savings schemes for securing some financial support for his daughters and then for himself in his old age. So the focus was never on the asset building but creating liquidity for meeting emergent requirements of his daughter's education or even their marriage. This fund he created over the years by meticulous planning and curbing expenditure on himself or his wife was perhaps the only thing left for Shyamlata to collect the twigs for rebuilding her nest. One more thing that he could do was to fix up a suitable alliance for settling Kamini. The boy was an Engineer and had settled abroad. Kamini's marriage had been fixed the next summer, barely six months away, when disaster had struck. Shyamlata had a lot of work to do. All her plans for a grandiose wedding had all but vaporized with the plumes of smoke from the pyre that had liberated Bindoo Babu's soul from the mortal remains of his body.

It just happens that when times change they continue in a trend. The woes of Shyamlata did not seem to end. Kamini's would be in-laws called on one day and while expressing sympathies were straight enough to call off the wedding on pretext of their boy opting out in favor of further studies. It was obvious that with Bindoo Babu gone, the expectant would be in-laws' too had little interest left in a widow and her three daughters. It was a shock for both Shyamlata and Kamini, but they had perhaps become steeled with the flurry of mishaps for feeling their own pains. They had instead focused on the younger two members of the family, both of whom were still to complete their education—Lata her class twelve and Kiran her eighth. Kamini had taken up tuition classes for school children and had started utilizing her science background for supporting her mother and sisters. Her own dreams had all just vanished. But her pain was not hidden from her mother. Both had their own reason for loneliness but Kamini's loneliness had far more significance.

Life trudged at a slower pace. Shyamlata's old house was now big enough for all of them. With little income from the funds that Bindoo Babu had left, they needed supplementary income to support their daily needs. So one morning they hung a "TO-LET" board on the side gate for renting out the two rooms on the back side. Bilaspur, a small town that it was, had little commercial or industrial activity. But it happened to be on the main railway trunk line and at a junction of two national highways and had a slightly hilly terrain with known coal deposits and a perennial river nearby. This was all that a local politician needed to put forth in his election campaign to get a thermal power plant sanctioned at Bilaspur. The coincidence of a formal notification by the government and the "TO-LET" board by Shyamlata brought Tarun, a young site Engineer posted recently for the Thermal Power Project to their doorsteps.

The doorbell rang and Kamini opened the door. A handsome young man around her age looked expectedly inside. "Yes, whom do you want to meet", Kamini asked with her beautiful eyes also asking the same. "Ma'm", Tarun pointed to the TO-LET board. "Ma", Kamini had called over her shoulder, not leaving the doorpost unguarded, "there's someone for the TO-LET". Shyamlata soon appeared, wiping her face with her cotton saree and invited Tarun in, "Come in, come in! Please have a seat. Go, get some water," she at once addressed both Tarun and Kamini. Tarun strutted in slowly and occupied the old sofa nearest to the door. He casually looked around to see the decadent old structure that was showing signs of neglect. For him it was a treat. Being a civil engineer, old buildings were of interest to him and he sometimes marveled the simple time tested strength of mortar and brick masonry with stone lintels on the windows and slabs for roofing supported by iron girders,. Roofs were usually higher than the present reinforced concrete structures and consequently cooler. "Hmm! looks just the thing I'm looking for. Just a dash of good paint after a thorough scrubbing and it will be ready for a comfortable stay with an old worldly charm", he thought to himself even as Shyamlata sat quietly watching him anxiously. Tarun's gaze roamed around the room and found itself suddenly caught in Shyamlata's gaze. He immediately collected himself and looked expectantly at her to begin the conversation. "The rooms are on the back side. Entrance is on the side of the road. Please have water and then you can have a look", Shyamlata said just as Kamini brought in two glasses of water on a steel tray. It was the first time that his eyes caught hers trying to cautiously absorb his persona as if weighing the genuineness in his attempt to take their two rooms on rent. Tarun sipped the water quickly and kept the glass back on the tray, now in front of him on an old center table. Everything from the approach, to the building to the furniture and even the two odd occupants seemed to be so out of world to him—enveloped in the silence that in itself was eloquent in prodding him to poke deeper, something he was not very sure of. He got up indicating that he wished to see the two-room set being offered for rental. Shyamlata nodded over silently to Kamini to guide him to the back side of the house, "I'll open the door from inside', she said while getting up.

Kamini walked silently a step ahead of Tarun, conscious of her own back being watched over by a stranger in her own house. Another day, it would have been the company of Manoj, who had for reasons unknown opted out of marriage with her, within days after her father had died. She suddenly found herself silently comparing Tarun's confident and mature disposition with that of Manoj who she had found a lively and carefree person, something she had liked instantly and something that she now wanted to forget. The duo reached the back yard where Shyamlata was waiting on a flight of stone steps in front of an open door. The courtyard was itself small but covered with a variety of floral shrubs and a few trees of guava and lemon that bore small fruits. He walked in behind Shyamlata, with Kamini now following him into the house. The rooms were not very large but were airy and accompanied by a miniature kitchenette converted out of a semicircular extension in the farthest room. A small toilet was attached with the front room. Large windows with fixed grill and mosquito net were provided with wooden door panes—all of which needed painting. The house appeared to fit in his immediate requirements, being a bachelor on his very first posting in a respectable government job that he had taken up immediately after finishing his engineering course. "What will be the rent like?" his first sentence since he had entered the premises. "Two thousand plus electricity and water charges", was the curt reply from Shyamlata," and no alcohol or late night parties. By the way who all are there in your family"? The rent appeared a little too high and Tarun had no family. Both these conditions were perhaps out of his reach for the moment. "Ma'm, I'm new to the place. I have come here for the Power Project. I'm alone. Will it be possible for you to make the two thousand all inclusive including one meal for me"? He had asked. Shyamlata said "well I can settle for two thousand two hundred for one time meal, but it will be strictly vegetarian—we are Brahmins". Tarun agreed and sought a week to bring in his luggage by depositing a months' advance rental. "Ma'm can you please get the rooms cleaned and painted at least in the meanwhile"? He had requested. Shyamlata had silently nodded. There was little she could do. Every penny counted and if this was the beginning, so be it.

Tarun soon moved in and settled. His work load was increasing every day with the project getting fast underway. Time flew and his presence in the premise had become a matter of fact security to the four ladies in the household. Kamini and Shyamlata busied themselves with whatever little they could do to generate income for making ends meet. Tarun had kept to himself, being busy during the day since early morning. When he returned in the late evening he found his dinner already kept on the kitchen slab in little casseroles. There was hardly any interaction other than his monthly remittance of rentals to Shyamlata which too was a formality of less than a minute at the door.

Days had turned to months and the monsoon settled in. It is often said that days are difficult to pass but the months just fly by. Shyamlata and her family sans Bindoo Babu had also limped back to a normal life that every human being goes through irrespective of any loss of near and dear ones. Shyamlata had started making use of her culinary skills in making pickles and sauces that she now started making on orders from nearby families. Kamini got on with her tuitions classes. Lata and Kiran were busy with their schools. The day ended with each one of them coming together in the evening when they all had tea in the front lawn while playing carom or badminton. One sweltering evening, Kamini was preparing tea for the family when suddenly her ankle twisted as she turned to fetch a cup from the side slab. In her attempt to balance she took support of the cabinet door handle just near the gas stove.

In her sheer ignorance, her *dupatta* dangled dangerously over the stove and soon caught fire and was engulfed in the flames. She ran out shouting for help. The women outside were more frantic with little effort to help out Kamini in the confusion. Just then Tarun entered from his side gate and heard the commotion. It was seldom that he ever ventured towards the front side. But today was different as the usual quiet was visibly absent in the conundrum and wails. He rushed towards the front portion and found Kamini caught in flames. Without losing time he jumped over the lawn hedge and in a swift movement with one hand snatched Kamini's burning *dupatta* from her body and trampled in with his feet to douse the flames, while holding her in his other arm to prevent her from falling down and hurting herself. Panic stricken Kamini had clung to him tightly and had just fainted out of fear and exhaustion. He had gently lifter her in his arms and led the wailing women inside to lay her on a bed. That was the second time he had entered the household. He had of course learnt about the untimely demise of Bindoo Babu and had felt a sense of sadness for the hapless widow who was struggling single handed. Leaving Kamini and the other's in the room, he rushed out to the refrigerator he had seen on his way in to get some cold water to bring Kamini to her senses. Soon she opened her eyes and caught Tarun looking intently. The others were all fretting around unsure of what to do. Tarun asked her gently, "Are you OK? Shall I get a Doctor? Fortunately you haven't suffered any burns. It was just that you fainted out of shock perhaps. Here just sip some water. You will be fine". Kamini just obeyed. She felt better from the cold sip of water and the breeze from the ceiling fan that was cooling her already semi wet clothes from the sprinkled water used to make her gain consciousness. More so the spontaneous care that a stranger had shown her had made her conscious of her own self. It had stirred in some sort of emotional catharsis that broke into a sob—perhaps the bottled up stress from braving her father's death, supporting her mother and broken dreams of a marriage that never materialized had all been poked too gently by Tarun's kindness. Sob turned to a cry and all the other ladies now suddenly charged forward as if woken from their slumber. Tarun quietly managed to slip out un-noticed to all but Kamini.

Back in his room he realized that today's dinner was over due to conundrum in the house and so he slipped out to the market nearby to get something to eat. It had taken him an hour to be back after a quiet stroll and a light meal. The metallic hinges of the side gate were noisy in the quiet of the night. As he slowly made his way to his room, he heard a soft female voice, unknown to him till now but something he had already made a mental connect with a persona that had intrigued him—Kamini. Yet it was Kamini. "Thank you. You saved my life. I could have got burnt severely had it not been for you. I just don't know what to say", Kamini said, as he turned back to face her standing in the shadows. It was then that her simple beauty had struck him for the first time. She had been the first one to open the door to him months ago. What had intrigued him had been the guarded composure with which Kamini always carried herself—something too serious for her young age and too strange for Tarun to understand. "It's OK, Just a natural act to help someone in distress. I'm sure you too would have done the same to anyone in such circumstances", he had humbly replied. Both were quiet for a moment, intently looking at each other in the dimly lit courtyard, their eyes speaking more than that was audible. "Well . . ." both broke simultaneously and stopped. Tarun recovered earlier from the pleasant coincidence," Please continue, you wanted to say something?". "No please. You speak first. I seem to have interrupted you", Kamini said softly with eyes now downcast with her feminine demureness.

"No, no!. It's just that I had been wondering to ask something from your mother but somehow it never happened. I felt that it may be treated as a trespass and not liked. But I was wondering how you manage it all alone? Er . . . I mean is there no one to help? Do you have some relative to be called upon, in times of need like what happened today? It's just chance that I came in when the accident happened. I mean it could have been really bad. You know! I had heard about your father from the neighbors but then that is just sketchy", Tarun was candid. Kamini stared at him for a moment as if weighing what to say. "We have no one here. My father died one morning leaving us all alone in this whole world. This is the only place where we could come back to. There are no relatives nearby. In fact none has even bothered to show up after the last rites fo my father were over. Even Manoj didn't wait long enough", she blurted. "Manoj?" Tarun queried. Kamini was speechless "What have I done? Why did I disclose it to this man? Who is he after all to be bothered about us?" she cursed herself silently while blankly looking at Tarun. "Oh! I'm sorry. It's just nothing. I'm fine. Thank you for all you have done. Here's some sweet pudding mother had made today. I'm sorry that we could not prepare the usual dinner for you", she had said in a single breath and then handing over the small steel container turned and walked away quickly. Tarun saw her receding figure and could sense that though she had not intended to, yet there was something she wanted to share. Her eyes had been expressive as if inviting him to probe more than what she actually wanted to state. Tarun shrugged and walked slowly back to his room. The pudding was delicious. Perhaps it had the touch of something more that the sweet that had gone into it.

Days passed. They had hardly spoken to each other after that little chat in the courtyard. But what had changed was the way they looked at each other. The earlier formality of strangers meeting had given way to a comfort that they both felt in each other's company. Shyamlata too had now become a little more open in that she would feel free to request Tarun for some odd help that she felt would require a male to do. Tarun had obliged. The mutual trust had begun to settle in and Tarun began to get invitation to family *pujas* and birthday celebrations. He found himself gradually being accepted as a family support. It only meant that he got more opportunity to see Kamini.

One day while returning from his office, as Tarun was getting down from the chartered bus that ferried the officers and workers to the project site, a large bull, chased by a pack of street dogs goaded and crushed him. He had sustained severe injury in his shoulder and back. People had rushed him to the nearby government hospital where the doctors had plastered his shoulder and advised him strict bed rest for three weeks. He was fortunate, they had said that his back had only suffered a minor sprain. It could have been serious. The treatment was appropriate but left him worried. His inability to even cook breakfast, manage his daily activities and more so the aspect of being locked up in the confines of his room on a bed unnerved him. He had asked the doctor of he could travel back home to Delhi, who had categorically said no. He could not even call his parents here who had no one else but themselves to care for. This was a situation that he had never even considered while coming here.

A couple of his co-passengers who had seen the accident happen had accompanied him to his room and left him comfortable on the bed. It was when Lata came for her usual daily visit to keep his food casseroles in the kitchenette that she was surprised to find his door open and discovered him groaning in pain. He had been back earlier than usual. She ran out and called Shyamlata for help. Soon all the four of them had gathered in Tarun's room asking him about the accident. Shyamlata appeared worried on seeing Tarun's condition. She had actually taken to like him over the period of his stay with them. She felt a little secure with him around. Probably, God had tried to mitigate their loss by sending Tarun as a support, she often thought. Strange are the ways of destiny for neither of them could otherwise have had a chance to meet ever, what of sharing a common house. Sitting down on Tarun's bed next to him she caressed his forehead like a caring mother and directed Kamini to get a glass of warm milk with turmeric powder dissolved in it, "it's a very good antiseptic. You will feel much better and recover fast from your internal injuries as well", she had said brushing aside Tarun's weak protests. Kamini was back fast with the yellowed milk. Shaymlata took it from her and fed Tarun herself—his right shoulder was bandaged and with the left he barely managed to prop himself amidst groans of pain. "What happened?", Shyamlata asked, as all others anxiously lent ears to hear. Tarun briefly narrated the incident ruefully adding the refusal by Doctor to allow him to travel back home. "Don't worry. We'll take care. You will recover fast with help of our homely remedies in addition to the pain killers. You can then go and meet them. Better still when you go, bring them over so that we can also express our gratitude to them for such a wonderful son who is very caring", Shyamlata was trying to perk up his morale. "And don't you bother—food is on the house. And one more glass of milk in the night", she said as they all made effort to leave him to rest. Kamini had a pained look in her eyes, something that was not hidden from Tarun. There seemed a longing that she wanted to share with him but was perhaps hesitant to broach. His thoughts went back to Manoj. Who was he?

A week had passed with Tarun managing his daily getting up and getting into bed with great difficulty. One morning as he tried to get up, he felt a shooting pain in his back. He tried to stand up but could not and instead fell down the bedside. Groaning in pain with a useless right shoulder he just could not manage to get up by himself. Just then Kamini entered with the usual morning tea cups—one for him and one for her that had become a routine since his incapacitation. Seeing his plight she immediately put the two cups on the side table and with all her strength that she could muster, helped Tarun back on the bed. She felt something warm on her arms. Tarun was crying—out of agony and his own helplessness. She felt touched and a sea of emotions poured out to a man she had grown to like secretly . . . Gently she helped him lie down on the bed and then again she lifted him by propping against pillows for sipping the tea. During the past few minutes, on more than one occasion they had become conscious of their own bodies against each other. Kamini sat in the chair next to his bed and passed him one of the tea cups. Tarun looked at her. Eyes downcast, her face was flushed with the effort and perhaps the warmth from their recent closeness. Suddenly he asked "Who is Manoj? Kamini was jolted out of her trance. She gulped her hot tea feeling the searing liquid burn her palate. She looked up with pain in her eyes, then calming down sighed and succinctly replied without much pretense, "We were to get married this year. They broke the proposal days after father's death". Tarun watched her closely for a moment and then keeping his cup down by his side, turned on his side slowly to hold her hand in his left hand. Gently pressing her hand he looked into her moist eyes and asked softly, "Will you marry me"? Kamini felt her heart miss a beat. Her face flushed, she got up with a start and ran out of the door only to run into her mother at the door post who smiled in a tacit agreement as if confirming her acknowledgement of Kamini's choice of the boy next door.

BOOK 2

Maya

. . . the limited, purely physical and mental reality in which our everyday consciousness has become entangled . . . Māyā is (*also*) held to be an illusion, a veiling of the true, unitary Self—the Cosmic Spirit . . .

Advait Vedanta Philosophy

CONTENTS

A ROUTINE DIVORCE

✟

It was a routine divorce proceeding, neither more acrimonious than that of the Kumar's where the philandering Mr. Kumar had been taken to the cleaners by his wife nor less than the one initiated by the scandalous Ms Chauhan who had proved that her husband's impotency had driven her into another man's arms & so impotency of her husband & not her adultery should be the ground for divorce. The court had been convinced by her competent lawyer & Ms Chauhan had robbed her husband of his dignity as well his last penny; though one was forced to admire her capacity for melodrama.

Today again a new case has come up & the stragglers are pouring in along with the interested parties & their witnesses. From experience he knew that this would be another long drawn battle for the lines etched on their faces looked like war paint & none of them was ready to give an inch.

He hoped it would be over soon in a few hearings though from experience he knew it was just wishful thinking on his parts. Sometimes he wondered why the long suffering spouses could not suffer a few more years by which time he 'Mr. Ghosh' would have safely retired & be sipping his favorite toddy in the hot afternoon without anyone bothering him. His wife mercifully had died before he would have to bear the ignominy of some other court reader typing down the sordid details of his sorry life.

'Take that down Mr. Ghosh' was how he had begun to refer to himself after serving in this same court for thirty five years now. They had tried to install a computer here & teach him to type but he had not been able to get the hang of it. One day he had deliberately broken the keyboard & the request for replacement or repair was still pending after two long years.

The couple standing before him today was like thousands of others he had seen. The lady was smartly turned up in pink shirt & black trousers while the husband looked approachable in his casually expensive blue shirt & khaki pants. Mr. Ghosh would have like to suggest to the lady that she appear wearing traditional outfits like sari or salwar suits which always made the court more sympathetic towards her though on his part Mr. Ghosh boasted that he had no biases & could infact always point out the guilty party correctly without his judgment being affected by a pink shirt or blouse.

Today though he was having difficulty in exercising his judgment. According to him the couple should not have been here in the first place. They kept exchanging glances which were neither scornful nor angry; instead he almost detected melancholy in the exchange.

They were in their twenties & seemed well educated with old money to take care of their Gucci shoes & Neiman Marcus outfits. The girl looked to be intelligent & not like the airheads who thought their father's money would see them through all the twists life had to offer. The boy had the snobbery affected by the rich which was enhanced by the rimless glasses perched daintily on his aristocratic nose. Both of them thought Mr. Ghosh make a real fine couple & he would not have minded sitting through a session of their marriage photographs. They certainly were the prettiest couple he had seen in the last decade & then it struck him; he had seen their faces peering out of yesterday's newspaper.

The boy was the heir apparent to the Singhania throne & the girl though coming from a middle class family was a management graduate from a reputed school where the two had met and decided to get married. The marriage had lasted for nearly a year during which time the jet setting couple had been photographed from the Swiss Alps to the Kenyan national park.

In between the newspaper reported they worked for the Singhania Empire with the girl also working on some important post. Money therefore did not seem to be a problem for the couple in front of him because obviously the boy was born with it while the girl had the brains to get a good education & snag a rich guy while at it, a feat she could repeat going by her still rosy complexion & perfect features.

She did not look like a gold digger also because her parents who were right then sitting in the courtroom were dressed up in normal clothes & not flashing diamonds like the parent in laws of Singhania corporation should. These people were grounded in reality & had brought up their daughter to respect it, so then what could have brought these people here thought Mr. Ghosh adjusting his ancient Remington which of late had started making noise similar to the one Mr. Ghosh's neighbor made early in the morning while clearing his throat.

Mr. Ghosh adjusted the ribbon & rolled the paper. The honorable judge took his place & the protocol of 'rise & sit' was followed. It was time to begin the proceedings & the wife's lawyer first addressed the court as the plaintiff. The address was routine citing incompatibility between the parties as reason for approaching the bench.

It was now the turn of defendant's lawyer to put his client's case forward & he all but agreed to the request for divorce. The honorable judge was in a mellow mood today after all as Mr. Ghosh knew she had just returned from London where she had gone to welcome her first grand child into this big bad world. She was not willing to let go off the case so easily.

She sat back in her chair without a word & for ten seconds there was pin drop silence. Then she lifted her hand & gave a wave to the plaintiff's lawyer to begin. The poor guy had not thought that the hearing would go beyond their opening statements today so he just fumbled a few sentences about how he would want another date. Normally the judge would have rebuked him for not coming prepared but today she quietly gave another date which was a month late.

Mr. Ghosh noted the date in the register & watched as the beautiful couple left the court. The remaining day was like usual & in the evening he took the bus which dropped him near his rented apartment.

He was still intrigued by the couple he had seen in the morning so he immediately went & dug out the evening paper where he had first heard about them. The ink print did not do justice to the soft beauty of the girl, the guy though looked aristocratic. Mr. Ghosh began to read the article once again but there was nothing which added to his knowledge. His curiosity was piqued & he had to get to the bottom of this affair.

'Why would two perfectly compatible people with both money & intelligence fall out?' he thought. In his heart of heart he had taken a liking to this magical couple who represented all that was good & beautiful in this world.

He waited for the next date of the court. The day dawned & before long the judge took her place. The two lawyers forewarned by their run in with her honor on the last occasion had come prepared with their case.

Surprisingly either side had no witness. The wife's lawyer droned on about how the husband did not pay attention to her & was busy with his work at all times. His client had entered into marriage for companionship which was missing from their relation for the defendant was busy expanding his parental business. His client too had the company's welfare at heart & worked hard at her job as proved by the profit margins of her department but she never brought work home. They had been married for almost a year but leaving aside the first couple of months the defendant had never taken a break from work with his client.

From the lawyers rambling Mr. Ghosh understood that this lady standing before him was starved for attention & this would not be the first time that such a case had come up before him. He knew the types though the early ones he knew had been philandering husbands with their interest lying somewhere else to pay attention to their wives. In our context being a workaholic was never reason enough to sue for divorce. Mr. Ghosh was beginning to revise his opinion about the sweet young woman standing before him; maybe her parents had not taught her to keep her expectations low. The girls these days were anyway getting out of hand & thought they could just change the thousand year old customs overnight. Mind you he was all for girl's education but they should look after the family too & the husband should always be the breadwinner. In that role the husband obviously would not have time to give his wife all the time & the wife should understand that.

This girl was not right in the head. Her lawyer was droning on & on, Mr. Ghosh allowed his mind to wander for the proceeding was becoming routine in nature & he had lost interest. He could type the minutes without listening to the lawyer's arguments.

Just when he was contemplating his dinner order for the day from banwari's restaurant & had finally settled on dal tadka with lacche parantha his reverie was broken by a sudden commotion in the courtroom. The girl's lawyer was holding a poster facing him, between his forefinger & thumb as if it was something sacred. He was marching towards the judge requesting for it to be deposited as evidence with the court. His expression said he was loathe to get rid of it & with decided reluctance he handed it over to the bailiff.

While Mr. Ghosh watched the scene unfolding before his eyes like a sequence from silent movie the baliff's pupils widened in appreciation. The reluctance which had clouded the lawyer's face now showed between the bailiff's bushy eyebrows & pencil moustache. His almost black lips curled in an O over his tobacco stained teeth. He looked stupefied which slowly changed to reverence.

He held it before himself & very slowly laid it face up on the honorable Judge's table. As Mr. Ghosh watched the expression on the otherwise stern face of Mrs. Dixit alias her honor changed to one of astonishment & then to anger.

(Routine Proceedings)

The girl had stood up at her place & was addressing the judge requesting permission to speak. The judge looked at the poster in front of her then looked up puzzlement writ large on her face but nodded her acquiescence for the girl to speak.

The girl began with confidence, 'Your honor, Ritesh my boyfriend of eleven months was speechless on seeing the heroine coming out of the water like a sea nymph in this turquoise bikini. Rightly so I would say as evident from the expression on the faces of all the men through whose hand this poster was circulated right now.'

She gave a studied pause & looked slowly at all the faces, her eyes coming to rest on Mr. Ghosh who held the glossy paper away from himself as if it would contaminate him. A small smile began to play on her lips & she continued 'On a whim he purchased the same bikini for me & I would not be boasting when I say I looked better than the actress or at least the bathers on Mauritius beach where we had gone for our honeymoon thought so. Six months of marriage & I have not gained an inch, my dietician & personal trainer would vouch for that. A month back I wore this outfit & took swim in our family pool. Ritesh was sitting besides the pool engrossed in some papers as usual. I stepped out of the pool & he looked up.'

With that she suddenly pulled down the zipper of her overcoat & let it fall back. The entire court including Mr. Ghosh let out a 'Wow'. A hush then fell over the courtroom with all eyes on the beautiful Ms. Singhania who would give any Miss World contestant a run for her money. There was a copper sheen to her body which glistened under the oblique sunlight falling from the skylight in an otherwise dimly lit room. The light held her in the spot & she gracefully lifted her hands over her head & did a twirl & while everyone watched mesmerized she picked up her abandoned overcoat & put it on. As she drew up the zipper a sigh went up in the courtroom.

Her voice now broke the silence 'Ritesh looked up from his papers & without changing his expression addressed me 'I think we should buy the equity being offloaded by

Lodha developers. It might come handy in the near future.'
Delivering this thought he went back to his papers. That
your honor is my case in a nutshell.'

Mr. Ghosh had sat shell shocked at the events unfolding
before his eyes. The girl was stunning if anything else &
this Ritesh was a fool to let her go. He Mr. Ghosh would
have waited hand & foot on such a beautiful woman. What
more she had guts to know what she wanted. Seeing her in
that turquoise outfit all the earlier bad thoughts about the
girl changed & Mr. Ghosh waited with bated breath for her
honor to deliver the verdict.

Her honor had recovered her composure & sharply
admonished the girl for her indecent behavior. She
immediately threw the case out of court & instructed the
girl to pay five thousand rupees as penalty for disturbing
the courts' proceedings. As for Mr. Singhania he was to take
psychiatric help from government appointed psychiatrist as
he was found to have lost touch with his natural instincts.
Everybody present in the court was advised not to discuss the
happenings outside for if found doing so they would serve a
month behind bars. Her honor did not want this proceeding
to set a precedent for young people to become as demanding
as their Western counterparts.

I am able to write this story for that very evening Mr.
Ghosh narrated it to me over his dal & laccha parantha
dinner which we had together in his house, after all I am
his neighbor & only friend. The day's events had struck him
dumb & it was after much cajoling that the story poured
out. The next day he went to the street market & returned

with a poster folded carefully under his arm. With help from me he pasted it on the ceiling directly above the pillow on which his head rested & the turquoise nymph now looked down at him from her perch.

A SHORT EXCHANGE

✟

Standing in the long queue for security check at six a.m. in the morning, I was drowsy & craving the warm bed I had been forced to vacate. At that moment I would have willingly kicked my career goodbye to be able to catch up on shuteyes. I lifted one heavy foot after another & unseeingly trudged after the blue blazer & black trousers in front of me. I took an extra step bumping my leg against his laptop & he turned around to growl but seeing my sleep laden face & swollen eyes decided to pass. I mumbled some apology & again bowed my head into the now familiar stance. The line was moving extra slowly today, the security had been tightened after the Mumbai attack & no one was complaining. I had plenty of time before my flight & my brain gone into sleep mode in the absence of any anxiety attack.

'You are taking the Jet flight to Mumbai', I heard a young male voice asking. Assuming the question was addressed to me I turned around to answer but found myself looking at the profile of a twenty-five something girl with nondescript features.

'No I am taking the Indigo flight', she replied noncommittally but did not turn back to face my face. I looked beyond her and spotted the owner of the male voice. A midheight average looking boy man, wearing a linen coat over a pair of jeans. Nothing much to hold my attention but my fuzzy brain had by now begun to clear & turning back to face the blue blazer & black trousers I strained my ears to overhear the conversation.

'You had come to Jaipur on a visit?' he enquired.

'No, my parents are here, I work in Mumbai.' There was a pause after which she continued,'You live In Mumbai?'

'No, I live abroad. I came to Jaipur to visit my parents. I spend six months here & six months abroad.' The obvious pride in his voice regarding his abroad base made me turn around once again though surreptitiously this time. I was right, there was nothing broad about him & the girl would be a sucker to get taken in.

'Where abroad?' she enquired eagerly. She was obviously a sucker.

'New York.'

'Wow, where in new York?'

'Upstate, New York.' he informed with studied nonchalance.

'Since when have you been working there?'

'Since 1995 no change that to 1992. Technically I have been living there since 1992. I studied there you know. And your whereabouts?' he posed.

'Malviya Nagar, Jaipur' she replied, trying to sound as if she had comprehended his question.

'No, I mean in Mumbai.' I could hear the smirk in his voice.

'At Parel.'

'No, no I mean whereabouts, your work.' I had been vindicated; this was no New Yorker but a phoney.

'With a Travel portal.' she replied though a bit diffidently. I felt sorry for the poor girl.

'Which one? Is it good? I want to know as in the US we refer to these sites frequently for cumpaarison.' No wait dear reader, I have not misspelt but merely put down comparison phonetically as uttered by that fake.

'Travelguru. Our forte is hotels & not flights though. But in case you want to book a five star hotel you should do it directly. Four & three star can be booked through portals,' she replied. Nice usage of words, I knew she was trying to recover lost ground.

'You know Sheraton & Hyatt are not five stars in USA,' his boasting was far from over.

'They are not!' she appeared flummoxed.

'No they are not five star hotels, merely four star,' he was reeling her in again.

'Which is a five star then?' she quizzed.

'Sheraton has good property here so it is five star but out there it is just four star.'

'Which is a five star?' she repeated.

'Hyatt in Delhi is a five star but out there it is a four star.'

'Which is a five star?' she asked again.

'Both Hyatt & Sheraton are what we call commodity hotels. We can book them using travel portals like yours.'

'That is a good idea, especially if you use *meta-sites* which display many options. Eases comparison & helps you get good deals like complimentary breakfast or extra night stay. What do you do?' she was on familiar grounds now & moving in for the kill.

'I am a developer with hotel industry.'

'Is 'Four Seasons' a five star hotel there?' she asked with pretend innocence.

'Hyatt & Sheraton are not five stars but 'Four Season's' is a five star hotel there.'

'I thought so.'

I did not need to turn around to see the knowing grin on her face. The battle had ended & we had a clear winner.

BENEVOLENCE

Ramji Neelkanth Brahma Pujarii was the name bestowed upon Bauji by his father who was the head priest at the temple in our ancestral village. The name was a mouthful & villagers shortened it to Ramya. To an urbanized outsider the shortened moniker would sound abusive but to the villagers this was a name given out of love.

Before our country got independence there was a surge amongst the youth to become barristers, following this trend Ramya too enrolled in the city to earn his law degree. One fine day he took the bus ride to the city with a small bundle containing his two clean shirts pressed carefully by his tearful mother & a half kg container full of ghee given by his father. He had money only enough to cover his fee and was to put up with a distant cousin who on his arrival in the city he learnt had moved away. How Ramya managed his accommodation & struggled to get his law degree till he retired as a High Court judge is another story. This tale here is about the munificence of Bauji alias Ramya.

Maybe it was the harrowing experience he had as a young person arriving in the city or it was the teachings of his parents & elders, whatever the reason, Bauji kept his doors open at all times for the villagers who traveled to the city in search of education or jobs. A room was always kept ready for these people. As he was a judge there was an army of servants allotted to him by the government who took care of these people.

Neela Aunty, his better half was on the other hand born & bred in a city. Her father had been a judge under the British Raj & she was used to being served besides having scarce knowledge of village life.

She was aware of her husband's fondness for his village people & though as a young bride she had protested vociferously against their arrival, she slowly mellowed down & adjusted her ways to accommodate the flowing mass of humanity.

Every time one of these villagers left, she would take inventory of the room & assess the damage. On the dinner table that day the conversation would begin thus, 'Ram, you know the bed-spread I had got from Calcutta,' she was the only one who called Bauji, Ram. Bauji would lift the soup spoon to his mouth, take a measured sip, lower the spoon in slow-motion to the bowl, raise his gaze, clear his throat, 'Uh!.' Neela Aunty knew from experience that this was the only response she would elicit from her husband so she would just rant along, 'There is a tear in one of the corners. The bumpkins tucked it so I would not know, but toady while changing sheets our maid brought it to my notice. I am glad she did, else I would have blamed her for it.' She would look expectantly at Bauji who would be busy heaping *sabji* on his plate. 'Uh!' he would utter because a pause meant, he was to acknowledge whatever had been delivered. Neela Aunty would then launch a scathing attack on the ill mannered people she had to put up with & how they were destroying all her carefully collected items.

Bauji had learnt to pay a deaf ear to these diatribes or even if they registered with him, he chose to keep quiet for saying anything in favor of his guests would be branded treason & Neela Aunty would go for him, hammer & tongs.

Now I had enrolled in the law college in the city but was not able to secure hostel accommodations. Bauji was distantly related to my mother. Upon urging by her, my poor father called him with trepidation. He need not have worried as Bauji was only too eager to have a young boy come and live under his roof while pursuing a career, Bauji himself held dear.

With a single suitcase containing all my possessions, I moved into the out-house of the judge's bunglow. The out-house had two rooms & during my stay there I saw a steady stream of people coming & going from the house to the room adjacent mine & then disappearing forever.

Neela Aunty was not overtly fond of me but as compared to the other irregular inhabitants she found me tolerable & in fact took me out a couple of times to get proper city clothes. I used to get up early in the morning to help Bauji with the gardening. He was an avid gardener & had all kinds of potted plants which he lovingly took care of. During the evening if he had a guest, he would point out all the various plants citing their botanical name, their use & significance. The security guards had been specifically instructed not to allow anybody to meddle with is green beauties. I was honored by being the only exception allowed to cater to his plants.

Three months had elapsed since I moved to the outhouse. There was a room vacant at the hostel & I had got it allotted to myself. Within a week I was to leave these gentle folks who had put up with me, when one day catastrophe struck. A man had moved into the adjacent room with his eight year old son. He was staying overnight & was to catch a train the next day for Haridwar. I heard a scream the next morning—it was nothing like I had ever heard before. I rushed out to see a distraught Bauji shouting at the guard. One of the pots had been vandalized during the night & the poor plant had been stripped of all its leaves. The guard was speechless and after much shaking of head & wringing of hands Bauji finally agreed to go into the house. The gardener who too had arrived by then was instructed to correct the situation & he mollified Bauji by confirming that the plant would live. The man & his son were nowhere to be seen & the guard confirmed that they had left earlier.

I got ready for college & as was my routine, went o the house to greet my hosts before leaving. To my utter surprise I found the otherwise serene Baujis raving & ranting about country bumpkins who did not know how to respect other people's property while the excitable Neela Aunty was coolly spreading butter on her toast. 'You know Neela, we should lay out some ground rules for all the visitors, you cannot trust these guards to be alert to every miscreant who has come in the guise of a guest. You please tell every visitor who comes here to stay away from the garden,' he shouted

'Uh', Neela Aunty muttered. I thought I detected a smile on her face.

FOREIGN TRIP

⚓

A travel discount offer to Malaysia, a second cousin who had set up residence in Kuala Lampur & been inviting him for a visit, children's school closure due to swine flu outbreak & of course a handsome bonus. All the ingredients required to travel with his family of three to Malaysia were ready.

For once in his life he did not dilly dally & called up the Tour & travel company on the phone number provided in the advertisement. 'Yes, he would visit their office today itself to acquaint himself with the offer details' he replied to the sweet voice on the telephone line.

In the evening he went to their office & a smart looking fellow who had exceptional marketing skills sold him the deal by throwing in one upgrade to first class in the Singapore Airlines. His wife did not drink & his children were still in school so that left only him to partake the single malts offered by airlines to its first class passengers.

On the designated date they flew to Malaysia where the dutiful cousin picked them up & installed them in his house. A local tour itinerary had been prepared for them which they stuck to for the next three days by which time being vegetarians they were thoroughly fed up of the sea food on offer. The cousin's kitchen came in handy & his wife cooked the meals for next three days to feed their entire brood including the cousin who was more than grateful for it.

He was almost grateful to land back in the country with its familiar smells, ineffective laws, clutter & people spilling from every corner. On reaching office he went to his cubicle. The peon who brought him his tea was the first to enquire 'Kaisa raha *phoreign, Saab?*' He nodded his head in a a gesture which meant good & you are dismissed at the same time.

He tried to catch up with the backlog on his table but during lunch which he had with his colleagues he was inundated by questions. Almost each one of them had flown the Malaysia, Singapore route, because the airfare & hotel deals offered by travel agencies was cheapest for this sector. They all had an opinion about their trips, though none of them even once said anything negative. 'Maybe I am not meant for foreign shores,' thought Arora ji to himself. He decided to downplay the trip.

'The trip was good & we saw all the sites worth seeing.' He replied to their queries but did not elaborate further. Not that he was very keen on sharing his travel experiences with anyone afterall it had just been a middle class Indian family taking the guided tour as recommended by the numerous brochures. They had not ventured off the beaten track to get some unique experience.

The excitement he had felt before leaving for the trip had abated forty eight hours after take off from the country & he had wanted to return even before the mandatory seven days were over. They had found their seats located in the middle row & he had seated his family there while going & sitting in the business class himself. The Malayan waitress had been too posh for him along with all his fellow passengers who were busy tapping on their computer screens & ordering single malts like he ordered tea i.e without any fanfare. The stewardess had pegged him as an upgrade & attended to him last. He too ordered a single malt but after that found it too tiresome to signal for her condescending attention once again. He had settled back in his chair & waited for the flight to land. At the airport they had found themselves fumbling with their Indian accented English at the custom check point.

The cousin had been waiting for them & that had been a welcome sight. They had gone to his bachelor's apartment where his wife had immediately got down to kneading flour & preparing dal, roti for her starving family & cousin. The latter had been only too glad to have home cooked meal served to him after months of noodles. Tours had been booked for the next five days which had passed too slowly. After the first day experience with noodles cooked in fish oil his wife had decided to get up early & pack lunches for the family to take along on the tour. Everyday they sat inside a McDonald & ordered coke which they drank with their parnthas. The sights were alright but then they had all agreed that India was better with its natural beauty & heritage.

Now back to the grind in the country he had put his holiday behind. Almost a week had passed since his return & everybody had all but forgotten his foreign trip. It was back to the vouchers & accounts at office with deadlines to meet.

Today he had to stop at the grocers to get lentils as ordered by his wife. It was late by the time he finished his work for the day but he still took a detour to make his purchases at their regular grocery store.

'Come Arora ji, it has been long since I saw you,' the lala sitting behind the counter asked solicitously. Arora ji was sure he addressed all his customers in this manner but today he detected an added sincerity in the Laljis tone.

Lala had money spewing from his ears. He came from a long line of banias who knew how to manage money & ensure that it grows exponentially. But Arora ji was richer for the experience after his foreign jaunt & the rich Lala seemed like the perfect sump for his knowledge.

For the first time Arora ji stated with pride, 'Yes Lalji we took a foreign trip, it was a short holiday to Malaysia.'

Lalji of course was not expecting this reply or for that matter any reply, so the expression on his face was suitably surprised which Arora ji took to be an encouraging sign. He launched into a happy concocted version of their seven day trip beginning with the comely, servile stewardess who fed him glass upon glass of single malt.

MOTHER, MOPED & ME

✝

'We should take this easy chair too, your father is at his vocal best while sitting in it,' my mother said even as she bustled around the flat they had occupied for almost thirty years. I imagined my otherwise reticent father holding forth on the economic policy of the government, as my mother continued her diatribe on the rising vegetable prices, neither of them ever listening to what the other was preaching. Over the years I had never witnessed either of them stopping to catch a breath.

I had been posted to Bangalore and the company had provided me with a two bedroom flat. The job came with enough perks to keep me from flapping my wings & flying away to other pastures. As an entrant to the world of corporate greed I was being treated like royalty which would soon turn to drudgery at the hands of cruel slave drivers. For the moment though I was happy & free. I was savoring this new independence, working hard & partying harder.

All this changed a month back. My father had to undergo a heart by-pass & I had to rush back home to be by his side. After a week of the surgery he was adamant that I go back to Bangalore & not extend my leave. I arranged with the hospital to have a full time care giver attend to my father & with a heavy heart went back. My heart was not into partying & I called them up at least five times a day to enquire about their health. Being an only child I felt all the more responsible. A month later I told them in no uncertain terms that they were coming to live with me. There were protests but I quashed all of them with the most compelling argument, 'I wanted to spend more time with them.'

Here I was now, helping them pack their lives of thirty years. My father was still not convinced about moving. In the privacy of the kitchen my mother confided that he thought they would be a burden on my young life. In his opinion, it is the responsibility of parents to rear their children & give them the best education to make them self sufficient. This is their duty & not an investment. The children should not be burdened with the task of caring for their parents after all they have a life of their own.

I broached this topic with my father over the chess board in the evening. A game of chess was our routine after tea time in the evening. In my absence my father substituted for me too. 'Papa, you are coming with me because I still need you.' My sentence hung in the air & after a minute during which my father pondered over his rook, he made his move & grunted in assent. I knew that grunt was meant as an acknowledgement.

The packing proceeded smoothly after that with my father supervising the packers & movers. We had decided to rent out this house, shifting all the furniture to the garage. Mother was in charge of identifying what would be required at Bangalore & what should be left behind. Back at Bangalore I had furnished only one room so most of the furniture was moving with us.

Some broken chairs, dining table, almirahs were being moved for safe-keep to the garage. Cartons containing old utensils, books & correspondence were being left behind for the rust & termites. I followed my mother to the garage carrying another heavy carton box which she had taped & marked identifying the items within. I wondered who would finally open these boxes or if at all they would ever be opened.

'Bablu, we should sell this old moped although your father is keen on giving it to the gardener. You know Lalaram, the one who puts in a monthly appearance to tend to the garden & charges for the entire month. Your father & he sit down & chat over tea for the entire hour that he decides to put in an appearance & now your father wants to give him my moped too,' fumed my mother. I knew Lalaram, he had taught me how to ride a bicycle & I too was not averse to the idea of him getting my mother's moped. What use was it otherwise & we would anyway get only a paltry sum for this relic. But I knew better then to impose upon my mother at this moment. It was better to wait for her to calm down & then present your thoughts to her disciplined school teacher mind.

This moped had represented freedom for her & disaster for me during my school days. Wrapped in her synthetic saree which was easier to wash & dry, my mother would prepare tiffin for me & my father and then both my parents would take out their two-wheelers to ride to their office. My school was on the way to the government primary school where my mother taught. I would lug my school bag on my shoulders, hang my water-bottle around my neck and then climb behind my mother. Her legs would spin the paddles of the moped & she would firmly state, 'hold on to me Bablu', upon which I would wrap my arms around her & we would be off.

As a child I had enjoyed riding behind my mother, feeling secure in her warmth. But things changed as I began to grow older. A few of my classmates taunted me, calling me Mama's boy and other names. I bore all this grimly but did not have the heart to tell my mother that I would take the public transport like my other classmates. I was in fifth grade & in my mother's eyes a child. I could not explain to her that I was a grownup who needed to deal on his own with his peer-group. One day though as I came to school one of the older boys who had a reputation of being a ruffian made a statement about the bra strap showing on my mother's back. Till that day I had never noticed this clothes malfunction. Being a middle class family mother had even maintained discretion with regard to washing & drying her undergarments. I had never so much as seen her under clothes anytime in the house. She hung them out to dry beneath a towel & even though it was my responsibility to gather the dried clothes & fold them in the evening after she had washed them in the afternoon. She made sure to remove her clothes from the drying line before I got there.

That statement sent me in a rage. I flew at the boy & knocked him down . . . He was bigger than me & after his initial surprise, picked himself up & gave me a sound bashing which makes me shiver even today. Some teacher had intervened & both of us had been sent to the principal. A phone call had been placed to my mother & she had come to the school to pick me up. I never told anyone as to why I got into that brawl. My mother gave me her silent treatment & next few days I had to rest as I had developed fever.

After that I had been adamant on taking the public transport to school. My mother had protested but father had intervened & I got my way. 'Go & tell your father to call Lalaram, it is better that he have the moped then to leave it lying around rusting. It served me well,' mother broke into my reveries. She stood besides the small lamb like vehicle caressing it lovingly.

PARANTHA & PICKLE

⚓

Crass could be the surname of the family of four sharing my compartment. The amazon sitting across me at the window seat had sired two brats who were literally sitting on top of me. The girl was a little monster & their pot bellied father sitting next to his wife encouraged her tantrums. She wanted to follow her brother everywhere including the washroom which meant the man had his crotch & belly at my eye level every fifteen minute.

The children if they could be called that littered the compartment with plastic wraps of wafers & other sweets. One empty bag floated across the air conditioning & landed on my lap spilling the remnants of wafers on my clean skirt. I glared balefully at the mother who had the decency to scream at the children. The father though immediately came to their rescue, 'They are just children, let them play.' He chose to be blissfully unaware, about civic sense and respect for other people's space.

Soon it was time for dinner. Before boarding the train, I had eaten a small snack & was not very hungry I immersed myself in my book. 'Children, do you want to eat,' the mother screamed loud enough for the engine driver to hear. The children were too busy devising new ways to ruin my journey they had no time to eat. The mother took out a paper box which contained oily paranthas & another plastic box that contained copious amount of pickle. The Neanderthals began to eat. It was the grossest display of table manners I had ever witnessed. The duo each held a parantha in their left hand & broke big morsels from it. The parantha would then be swept around the pickle box to gather oil & masala, with a switch of hand it would be chucked towards the gaping moth where it landed after completing a perfect parabola along the flight path. The mouth would then begin to masticate it. I was fascinated by the display. It was like watching a family of stray cows chewing on their cud.

The girl meanwhile decided she wanted to come down. The father asked her to wait till he had finished eating but that did not have any impact. The child started bawling. I began to dread the crotch in my face & got up to stand in the aisle. 'Can you please help her down,' requested the mother. I had no choice but to help the little girl down. She immediately proceeded to grab a parantha from the box & began to chew vigorously. The parents looked on indulgently & the mother rolled p some pickle between a parantha & got up to hand it over to her son.

For next few minutes the munching sounds kept pace with the *klicty-klack* of rail wagon wheels. I tried to immerse myself in my book but the noise was too overpowering.

Looking across the aisle I found my disgust mirrored in the eyes of lady sitting across. We shared a smile.

The litter around my feet kept growing. After half hour the family had stopped chomping & started packing their food. I stared hard at the lady & then stared down at the plastic wrappers strewn around. She got the message & bent down to pick the litter. Her husband immediately reacted, 'Let it be'. He pushed the litter with his foot, below the seat. I exchanged another glance with the couple sitting across the aisle. The pot belly now got up & with his errant daughter in tow proceeded to the washroom. The mother wiped her greasy fingers on a handkerchief. She took out a bottle of soda & with her fingers still glistening with pickle oil, uncorked the bottle & put it to her mouth. A burp followed.

The family across now opened their dinner & proceeded to lay it out elegantly on paper plates. The lady exclaimed, 'You forgot the vegetable tiffin.' There were nice chapattis & cake pieces lying on the plates but there was no vegetable to accompany the chapattis. Meanwhile the pot belly returned with is daughter & on overhearing the couple's distress instructed his wife to hand over the pickle box to his travelling companions. 'Brother, take some, this is good home pickle. Do you want some *bhujia* too'?

The man declined but pot belly would have none of it. He scooped out a large helping of pickle & heaped it along with garlic bhujia on one of the plates. The couple thanked him profusely but he shrugged it off, 'Bhaisaab, this is our culture. We should help one another.' Then he suddenly looked in my direction. By now the hunger pangs had begun to hit me too. The sweet sour smell of pickle wafted through my nostrils, scrambling my brain. I am sure my eyes were moist with hunger.'Here you too have some parantha & pickle,' the man extended two paranthas covered with pickle to me. I thought of his unwashed hands holding the parantha rolls. But hunger got the better of me, after declining once out of courtesy I accepted the rolled up paranthas & began stuffing myself. The food was heavenly.

The lady across the aisle started talking to the couple's daughter. I retreated behind my book & so did the gentleman sitting across the aisle. An hour later the train stopped & the gruesome foursome got off. Telephone numbers were exchanged with promises of catching up & the four departed from our compartment. The lady let out an audible sigh of relief, 'What a disgusting family,' muttered the lady masking a burp with the back of her hand. There was a strong smell of pickle oil, digested parantha & something else—something which smelt like ungrateful snobbery.

POMEGRANATE

✝

'Mridula, you are not giving pomegranate juice to Kavi,' my mother's tone was accusatory. These days she was always finding fault with me. If Kavi developed diaper rash, it was because I was too lazy to make him wear cotton undies & used these plastic diapers which irritated her grandchild's' skin or if he had a runny nose it was because I did was too busy to make vegetable soup for my child & instead depended on medicines. Kavi was now fifteen months old & a healthy child but my mother was not satisfied. She doted on her first grandchild & was constantly busy in the kitchen making some concoction or other to make Kavi healthy, as she claimed.

Pomegranates were a thing for my mother. Back when I was young, I remember her sitting on the dining table with a few pomegranates & patiently peeling away the hard outer skin, detaching the red pearly arils by putting pressure with her thumb. Neither a single aril was allowed to escape, nor was a drop of juice wasted. It took her a good half hour to have three bowls of pomegranate arils ready for us siblings to consume. She never saved any for herself & papa was always away, so it was only three bowls. As I grew up I took to bringing in a fourth bowl which we siblings would fill from our share & give to her. I distinctly remember the first time we gave her the bowl full of pomegranate. She got tears in her eyes & then forcibly took each of our bowl & emptied a few arils from hers into ours till only a few were left for her to consume. 'You are children & need the energy, so eat up. I am old and no longer need the pomegranate juice,' with that she had wiped the tears from her eyes.

Now I don't ever remember her getting emotional about mangoes or bananas or even apples. The latter was costly if not pricier than the pomegranate but mom never shed tears on a slice of apple. The banana agreed was a poor man's fruit & she never even pulled up Meena bai if a banana went missing occasionally. Mind you she always kept a count of numbers of bananas, apples & mangoes. Regarding apple & mangoes she was more vigilant & Meena bai also was aware of the fact so the latter never went missing though once in a while, mother herself gave a couple of them to Meena bai to take home to her children. Mother had always been generous but when it came to pomegranate it was another story. She would not partake of even a single seed leave alone an entire fruit.

Morning she would allow her tea to get cold but painstakingly peel the pomegranate for us children. In my later years I had often wondered about this duality in her nature & had labeled her a miser too. In my college days while under the influence of Guvera & Lenin, I had thought my mother to be a capitalist and of the worst sort.

After my marriage with the responsibility of running a household I had begun to see the wisdom of my mother's ways though I still thought that if the maid's helped themselves to some fruit & grain occasionally It would be better to ignore it rather than bring things to a head. A maid was more precious than a pomegranate and I was a busy career woman. Although this argument did not hold good viz a viz my mother who too had also been a lecturer in a government college which was located more than 50 kms from our town. Every morning she took the eight am bus to that remote college & reached home only around seven pm. With the added commute hers had been a tougher life but still never did a pomegranate aril vanish under her vigil.

With Kavi making an entrance I had temporarily put my career on hold & taken a yearlong sabbatical, half of which I had spent at my mother's place which was in the same city. Under her strict diet regime, I was back on my feet in a week. She made ladoos for me which tasted like heaven, morning evening there would be glass of milk, afternoon there would be lime water & a milk shake besides all the regular meals. I dreaded stepping on the weighing scales after a month but she assured me that I needed this diet. After six months I vowed off her ladoos upon which she insisted I have two fruits daily. With the exess weight I did not want to eat bananas so she took to peeling a pomegranate for me every day. Watching her wrinkled fingers scoring the fruit I was filled with affection for my dear mother. Here was a labour of love. She would crush a handful of arils & administer the juice to Kavi, advising me that it was good for his health so I should continue giving it to him.

Year later, when I joined the job stream again, a maid was hired to look after Kavi & as instructed by mother, I advised the maid to peel a pomegranate daily & give the juice to Kavi. Some of my mother's trepidation had rubbed on to me. Santosh the teenager hired to take care of Kavi was instructed to come by 8 am & on her arrival the first thing I did was to hand over a pomegranate, a bowl, an old newspaper & a knife to her. While I scurried about getting the house ready for the day & preparing to leave for office, I watched Santosh peeling the pomegranate. Once she was finished I would take a handful of seeds, put them in the mixer, strain the mixture into Kavi's juicer & put it in the refrigerator with instructions to Santosh to ensure it was given to Kavi in the afternoon. Rest of the arils would be put in a bowl on the breakfast table for consumption by me & Vikram.

I used to pat myself on my efficient system & with temerity even advised my mother to follow suit. She declined at once asking me instead to not become too complacent as the girl would certainly be consuming the arils without my knowledge. With disdain I had replied, 'So what if she consumes, a few, we can afford it.' Mother had kept silent upon that. Her words though continued to disturb me. Next morning I sat at the dining table from where i had a clear view of the kitchen, Santosh was sitting with her legs crossed in front of her on the floor & peeling the fruit. Every once in a while a bunch of arils would roll on to the newspaper which she would pop in her mouth. Once she finished peeling, she wiped the knife with the edge of the newspaper, got up with the bowl in one hand, took a handful of seeds & put them in her mouth. The bowl was then put in the refrigerator, knife picked up & put in the sink while newspaper & peels stowed away in the dustbin. I was furious, I fed this girl from my own table, never grudging her anything, in fact in the one month that she had been with us she had put on a couple of kgs and started glowing. The ungrateful wrench, nothing was ever enough for them, they will always steal from you.

Vikram had left for his office so I waited for the evening & then discussed the incident with him. He was reasonable & realistic as always. 'Look Mridu, we have found this girl to look after Kavi, with a lot of effort. We will have to hold on to her till we can find a replacement, If you tick her off for consumiong a few pomegranate seeds she might take out her angst on Kavi or maybe even leave our service under some pretext. You will have to reign in your temper after all it is only pomegranate arils, we can afford it.' I reared like a snake whose tail had been stomped upon. 'It is not about us being able to afford it. I give her fruit to eat so why does she have to steal.' Vikram smiled, 'You do not give her pomegranate. It is the forbidden fruit therefore more tempting. Incidentally some scholars believe that your pomegranate and not poor apple might have been the forbidden fruit consumed by Adam in the Garden of Eden.' With that useless bit of information imparted, Vikram considered the chapter closed & turned to his laptaop. I could not close it so easily.

Next morning, I got up a wee bit early & after brushing my teeth & preparing tea for myself, brought in a old newspaper, bowl, knife & the pomegranate. I t took me half hour that first day to peel the fruit & clean up afterwards but I was satisfied. Vikram came out from the bedroom, saw my endeavor, turned his gaze skyward & without a word went into the kitchen & got his tea. He knew better then to argue with me. In the bargain I reached office late, earning dark looks from my colleagues & a Q&A session from my boss. I vowed to get up half hour early from next day onwards. The resolution lasted for two days after which I became my boss's punching bag every morning on account of my tardiness. How could I explain my pomegranate plight to him? I scoured the internet & picked up a few tricks on how to peel the fruit with minimum fuss. I cut the pomegranate horizontally & tapped it over a bowl with a heavy wooden spoon, the arils dropped beautifully in the bowl, on the tablecloth, rolled out to the ground, squished under my slippers & finally the spoon slipped out of my hand, clattered on the floor waking up Kavi. Santosh came in & saw the disaster, I asked her to tidy up the mess. Feeling a tad guilty I tried to explain my action to her,' I wanted to save time but look at the mess I have created instead.' She *tcch-tcched* and went about cleaning. 'Didi, this is the apple season, maybe we should grate some apple & feed Kavi after all he is teething & needs the strength' she stated. I looked for hidden meaning in this simple statement of fact. Was she mocking me or maybe trying to provide me a way out. I had no way of knowing but her idea seemed good. 'Okay, there are a few pomegranates left in the refrigerator that you peel tomorrow after which we shall switch to apples.'

Next morning, Santosh arrived on time & without being asked, took out the pomegranates from the refrigerator. I sat at my vantage seat on the dining table, sipping my tea while she rind the skin, pushed out the beautiful arils with just the right amount of pressure & popped a few in her mouth without any show of pretense. Mother would never have given in like his.

QUID PRO QUO

✛

'Who gave you this shirt?' Shaina asked, spotting the 'Armani' box carefully tucked under the passenger car seat. Nikhil mentally kicked himself then replied curtly, 'Why, cant I buy anything for myself?' 'Well, it is not your taste, you generally stick to casuals and sportswear. So, who gave it to you?' Women & their indisputable logic, thought Nikhil, 'I bought it, on a whim.'

That should have ended the conversation but, Shaina was like a street dog with a juicy bone after days spent hungry. She would not let go off it even if it meant roughing it out against an entire pack. Here was Nikhil alone & defenseless. 'I do not buy that argument you are not somebody to act on a whim. I have been married to you for seven years now; I would know about your urges or the lack of them.' She never missed a chance to snub him. Yesterday he had declined her offer of a romp in the bed because he had been too tired after the day's work, this was the fall out. She was looking at him expectantly, even after so many years spent driving alongside, her stare still disconcerted him, but he would stop only at his own peril. 'Why are you staring at me?' he asked defensively. 'There is sweat on your brow.' His left hand unwittingly reached for his brow even as he heard her tittering. This was too much for him, 'What is your problem, can't I buy something for myself without you becoming suspicious? I brought it a few days back, at the Delhi Airport where I was waiting for my connecting flight to Chennai.'

'You are lying again, yours was a domestic connection, Armani showroom is only in the International lounge,' she barked this time. Nikhil mentally kicked himself, 'I should have remembered that, after all she had accompanied me on numerous trips via Delhi and knew the Airport layout as well as I did.' In truth lay his redemption he decided, 'Alright, a new trainee gifted it to me for mentoring him in our department.' 'You think, I will believe that, Even a seriously retarded person would not buy that story. Why would you lie to protect a male trainee? I bet it some young nubile girl with stars in her eyes or ambition in her blood who has got your trousers in a bind.' 'Stop being vulgar Shaina,' Nikhil barked even as he deftly maneuvered into their apartment block. The security guard saluted & also waived from them to stop. Nikhil rolled down his window & the guard extended a parcel. It was from an online—internet shopping store.

Shaina excitedly reached for it. Nikhil was glad to pass it on to her, the parcel had drawn away attention from his Armani Shirt at least. They took the lift to their apartment & Shaina went into the kitchen. She came out holding the parcel & a pair of scissors.

Nikhil went to the washroom & on coming out saw her standing in front of the full length mirror in a grey blue dress made of a gossamer material which hugged her curves, making her look sexy and feline. He at once wanted to take up her yesterday night's offer. 'It looks good on you, in fact it makes you look sexy', Nikhil said aloud. It was how he felt. 'You should wear dresses more often. Let us go out to your favorite restaurant in this dress tonight,' he was trying to make her forget the Armani as well get her in the mood, she looked alluring in the strappy shouldered, see through material. 'I am tired, we will eat at home,' with that she started stepping out of the dress & into her house kaftan. Nikhil turned away at the sight of her undressing, from experience he knew it would be a tough night, he would not get anywhere with her instead there would be brickbats. He picked up the packing material lying on the dining table & glanced at the price tag. 'Whoa, Shaina this dress cost twelve thousand bucks.' 'No Nikhil this dress cost eleven thousand & seven hundred bucks for which I paid out of my pocket & not had it gifted by a trainee.'

The barb stung, it was time to retreat. 'I will be wearing it to my magazine annual dinner. You may come if you can take away time from your mentoring session.' 'Shaina! stop behaving like that. It was just a gift. If you want I will return it.' 'Don't bother,' that was her way of ending an argument.

On the night of the dinner, Shaina handed him a box. It was an Armani again. Nikhil glanced at her face to check her expression. 'I exchanged that shirt, did not like the colour, it would not suit you, try this instead,' she stated deadpan. Nikhil obligingly put on the shirt. She was right as usual. This shirt looked good on him, he only hoped Anisha would not ask him to wear her gift some day. It was too early in their relation so he was relatively safe from pestering from that end for the time being at least.

On reaching the venue they were greeted by the editor-in-chief, Deepak Kalra, who was ushering in all guests. 'So how is my most talented writer,' he pecked Shaina on both cheeks & shook hands with Nikhil. 'I am good,' replied Shaina demurely.'You are looking good too, had your husband not been around I would have said yummy enough to eat. This dress is looking good on you.' Nikhil thought he saw a look exchanged between the duo & started to feel peeved. Deepak took his hand again, 'You are one lucky guy, you both make a good match & that Armani sits well on you, suits your personality I would say. Shaina knows how to dress you.' 'Yes, she has good taste,; Nikhil replied tilting his head inward to suggest he meant himself as the taste in question.

'Of course,' Deepak patted his shoulder as if in appeasement & then continued, 'it is reflected in her poise, her gestures, her dressing style. She makes every things she wears look good. I know girls & believe me I know some who can take a twelve thousand dress look like it is bought off fashion street whereas Shaina can even make a street shift look like designer wear.' Nikhil glanced pointedly at Shaina, who was soaking in the praise. 'Yes, that is our Shaina, who buys twelve thousand worth dress over internet knowing fully well in advance that it would fit her like a glove & she would look stunning in it.' Shaina looked at him directly then turned her head in Deepak's direction, 'it is my mentor who has taught me,' with that she waived at somebody in the crowd & left the two men, embarrassedly staring at each other.

THE WINNING POINT

✠

I had stepped out to grab a bite at the nearby south Indian restaurant, as the office canteen did not open on Saturdays. We had a five-day week but most Saturdays I came to office. In the beginning as it was actually to catch up with the paper work but slowly as I became more proficient & consequently bored the paperwork just became an excuse to avoid spending 48 continuous, tedious hours at my residence with the wife & children.

The staff at the restaurant waited for me on Saturdays because I would order coffee for the entire staff consisting of three waiters, two cooks & one receptionist after my regular meal of a rawa masal dosai plus a plate of steaming idlis. The restaurant was some distance away but across the street from our office; one of them would usually spot me the moment I stepped out & the hot idlis would be waiting when I opened the restaurant door; the dosai took a bit more time but meanwhile I could feast on the idlis.

Though I had been coming to the same place at least four times a month for the past four years yet they would wait for my order before preparing coffee for everybody. On most of these afternoons I was their only customer as my office was located in the business part of the town with most of the surrounding offices having five-day week populated by employees who definitely had more exciting family lives.

Today I was surprised to spot somebody sitting with his back to me on my favourite table; where the streaming sunrays sun rays made for a cosy bench on this cold winter day. I chose to sit next to the door & immediately the idlis were placed before me. I began to eat & the rawa dosai too appeared. I finished eating & than ordered the usual round of coffee when the man whose back was facing me got up to leave, I bent my head low so as not to avoid catching his eyes, my social skills were nothing to be proud of. A few seconds passed & I heard a booming voice overhead "Dilton".

This address bought my head up & but for my left hands quick reflex I would have spilled the coffee all over me, for this I will be eternally grateful to my left hand. There towering above me stood 120 kgs & 6 ft 3 inches of Shikhar. His mother must have been a woman with forsight for naming him thus. We had been schoolmates & had always been competing against each other for the first position but whereas learning facts & figures came easy to him, I had to stay awake for hours in the night to retain my first position. He was with the school basketball team too & generally a popular guy. On the other hand my classmates with reservation would approach me & only when they had a particular problem with some subject & Shikhar was busy elsewhere.

Before he joined our school there had been no competition for the top slot but only for the second & balance positions for I had established my supremacy in that slot. Shikhar joined our school in the mid session when I was in class 9th & in the half yearly exams which took place less than a month after he joined I was amazed to see that there was a difference of only 3 points between him & me in the exams. First time fear struck, this tall gangly good-natured boy who even played basketball had come so close to usurping my reign, which had held steady for the past 8 years. I was shaken to the core & there & then decided to put in an extra hour of studies everyday. My first position was my only identity without which I would sink into the whirlpool of acne & gangly limbs in no time.

Thus it remained for the next four years till we completed our secondary exams. On all but two occasions I stood first & these two times also I would have retained my position but first time I came down with mumps which pushed me to the second slot & in the consecutive exams too the mumps or should I say the last result left a depression which again made me slip to the second slot. In the final exams though I was ready for a fight & I studied everyday till I developed a persistent headache but it paid off & I was the topper again. But in this particular year while I was battling mumps & Shikhar, fell the silver jubilee celebrations of our school.

We were in the 11th standard than & since the 12th with their upcoming boards were barred from participating we were the senior most class. All the big wigs of the city had been invited & a grand play was to be staged directed by a theatre personality who had been called all the way from Delhi. In this play a '*Sutradhar*' was required, somebody to connect the various scenes together by narrating the uniting threads between the various scenes & doing all this while moving around the stage.

The director asked our class who all would like to do it & at least 15 of us lifted our hands. He made us all read a passage & than short-listed eight of us with Shikhar & me included. Now he asked each one of us to go through the passage silently & than come out to the front of the class where we were to read it aloud with expressions although we need not know the passage by heart. Eight of us & the director would then grade each on a eight point scale & the one who had the highest total would perform the role. One by one each one of us gave our performance. Only Shikhar & me had been able to learn the passage by heart & performed without the text in hand, here I must admit that Shikhar was good & with his gangly frame he looked the part too. Time came for all of us to give the grades. I put myself on top, Shikhar next & the other six in some sort of sequence behind us. The director took the sheets from us & 15 minutes later after totaling up the scores from individual sheets announced the score. I had got the part though Shikhar was to be my understudy as he had placed second with a difference of only one mark.

On hearing the announcement I felt a stab of guilt for in my heart of hearts I knew he had performed as well if not better than me & it might have been only because I had marked myself highest that I had got the part. I quickly brushed the guilt away or so I thought & immersed myself in the rehearsals. On the anniversary day the crowd gave me a big round of applause & I was even asked for an encore of one of the passages. I was thrilled, than I caught sight of Shikhar applauding as loudly as others in the wings. I took my bow & left.

Another year passed & we moved to different colleges. I proceeded to do my engineering from a prestigious college after which I joined a MNC. Today after 10 years here I was meeting him again. He had not changed much though the & had a carefree expression about him. He hugged me & I too clamped my arms around his broad shoulders. I suppose I managed to say all the right things for he still had the happy expression on his face fifteen minutes after having met me. I learnt he too had done his engineering & was with a government department. He was posted at Delhi & had come here on a tour. He had a daughter & had been married for 4 years. It did not come as a surprise to me that he had had a love marriage & his wife was working too. You can predict these things very early. I told him about my arranged marriage & two children.

I invited him for dinner in the evening to meet the wife & children but he declined stating that he would bring his wife the next time round. Then the two families would get together moreover he had to catch his train at 7 p.m. which meant no dinner though he would be happy to have a couple of drinks in the evening with me before leaving. I agreed & named the club of which I was a member, a perk of the company I worked for. We agreed to meet there at 1730 hrs as the railway station was also close by & we would get an hour together.

We parted ways, as he had to reach his office to gather some papers. I went back to the office to finish whatever irrelevant thing I had been doing & after an hour picked up my car & drove home. The wife expressed neither pleasure nor surprise at my early appearance though the children were glad to see me. I told her that I had met an old friend & would be again leaving for the club to have a couple of drinks with him. She asked me who it was & I gave her a sketch of how & where we had met now & earlier. I stepped into the shower to avoid the questions she was dying to ask & left immediately to pick up Shikhar from his guesthouse. On the way to club we exchanged views on politics & government, information technology & preity zinta.

We reached at 6 p.m. & after settling down ordered our drinks. I asked the manager to check up with the railway station to see whether the train was on time & than relaxed on the easy chair. The patiala pegs soon loosened us up & I would like to think inebriated us for now I don't recollect who raised the topic of that play. I asked him whether he had truly liked my performance & he stated it had been good but he would have performed better. After some good-natured raging I asked in an off-handed manner how he had graded himself amongst the eight finalists. He candidly admitted he had put himself first & me second.

In that moment I felt a physical weight lift of me & on an impulse hugged him. He was surprised but hugged me back; I caught the club manager's eye gesturing at his wristwatch. I saw it was time for us to leave in order to catch the train. I told Shikhar this & we both got up, I felt light & wobbly, it could be because I had had one drink too many.

THE DIARY

✜ ————

His mobile rang in the middle of the night. He wanted to ignore it but the persistent ringing was did not allow him to do so. He eventually picked it up & sleepily growled into the speaker, 'Hello.'

'Siddhartha Beta,' it was his mother in law on the line & she was sounding very distraught.

He was suddenly wide awake, 'Yes Ma, what is wrong.'

'Beta, Maya took the intercity from here for Delhi. We just got a call that there has been an accident & two bogeys have toppled over. Her father has already left for the railway station for more information. Please do something,' she broke down & started sobbing.

His heart gave a lurch, his wife was in an accident, he controlled his voice & told his mother in law to calm down.

Putting down the phone he sat in a daze & then called Abhinav, his school buddy who too had settled in Delhi & was now a family friend.

Rati picked up the phone & hearing the panic in his voice put Abhinav on the line immediately. He told Abhinav what had happened.

An hour later both of them drove to the accident site. With mounting panic losing to hope as they drew closer to the accident site, Siddhartha was in tatters & it was Abhinav who went to the police personnel standing there. They directed the duo to the nearby hospital. As the first ray of sunshine dispelled the last remnants of darkness, a permanent gloom settled over Siddhartha. His Maya lay covered in blood on a dirty stretcher in the morgue.

It was a nightmare from whose clutches Siddhartha found himself unable to escape. There were people sympathizing with him. He had to console Maya's parents who looked shattered. The sad & bereaved kept thronging in their house for innumerable days till finally Siddhartha decided to shut them out.

Only Abhinav & Rati were welcome as they had known Maya almost the way he had. Six months passed thus till one day a boy from Maya's office delivered a carton box along with a substantial cheque at their residence.

Before going to bed he decided to open the box. There was a silver photo frame showing them sipping pinacoladas under beach umbrellas in Goa. I had been a memorable holiday & Maya looked tanned & relaxed.

Next came out a yellow cloth envelope into which someone had carefully put all sort of nick knacks. There was a pearl comb which he had never seen Maya wearing but it smelled of her hair.

A graphite pencil with a snoopy mounted at the other end came next. He could picture Maya stooping over her desk, lines of concentration on her forehead, constantly flicking the pencil to hit her bowed head with the other end. He had observed her in this stance while preparing the house accounts. Earlier in their marriage he had playfully caught the pencil which had really angered her. He remembered going out that evening to the stationary shop & purchasing a foot long pencil with a rubber toy at one end. He had pasted a note on it which 'So you may not hurt your pretty head.'

Her eyes had brimmed with tears & she had apologized profusely. It had been so easy to love her then. Gradually life & routine had caught up with them. Carefully laying down the pencil he dived into the yellow envelope once again & drew a delicate silver anklet. Maya had been very fond of silver jewellery & anklets were her all time favorite. She liked the tinkling sound of the anklets but had been forced to remove the bells as office decorum did not permit it. This anklet though had its bells intact. He emptied the contents of the yellow bag on the bed but could not find the pair.

Spreading the contents he found a wine cork on which a heart had been drawn in black ink between the letters A & M in red. Siddhartha suddenly began to feel queasy. The paraphernalia in front of him was disturbing his senses. It all belonged to Maya as per the office but this was a Maya he did not know. There was a wooden paper cutter bearing the legend 'I am cut in half'. The writing was not Maya's.

He gathered all the items & put them back in the yellow bag. He felt the need for a drink & poured himself a glass. He sat in the drawing room & commanded his brain to conjure up memories of happy times. But his brain refused to comply. Instead it brought back the last fight they had. She wanted to go to the office on a holiday while he had made plans & booked the sauna at the club. In the end he had gone alone. They had more then their share of fights & while she had labeled him a typical Indian Male Chauvinist he had called her an ambitious bitch who would go to any extent to advance her carrier even ignoring her home in the process. After the initial one year, the bitter tussels had all but overtaken their life till it had become their only means of communication.

His glass was empty, his wife was dead & here he was thinking about bad times instead of respecting her memory. He got up to go back to the bedroom where lay the trigger.

There was something lying at the bottom of the box. He lifted out a thin diary made of handmade paper. This was Maya's handwriting as he knew it. There were entries made at infrequent intervals. Maya had not been much of a writer for each of these entries was not more than a paragraph long.

She wrote about their Goa holiday & how he had carried her piggyback to the hotel from the beach. That day she had taken one too many. She described it as riding away into the night on her beloved trusted mount. It was quite romantically humorous.

One entry described the cozy luncheon shared with an 'A' where they had sipped a rose wine. She admitted to her growing fondness for 'A' & his reciprocity. That is where the cork memento came into being.

Many of the pages were dedicated to her growing disenchantment with Siddhartha. Those pages painted him a villain who was not at ease with woman's emancipation & who wanted to stunt his wife's growth.

The anklet & comb were not accounted for in the diary but there were other sundry incidents in which she described her confusion & setbacks. On one page she wanted to renounce the world & on another she wanted to spread her arms & encompass it. Siddhartha felt a dark seething anger growing in his belly. He ripped the pages of the diary & flung them

Here was a Maya who had existed without his knowledge. He had wanted to know her every pore, every fiber but not necessarily understand it. Knowing her meant he was in control of her but Maya had vanished even prior to the accident. She had lived two lives & while he mourned the one she had shared with him, it was her other life which intrigued him.

Her death had revealed the existence of her other self, but she had taken it to her grave, leaving behind the knowledge that Maya had existed without Sidharth too—knowledge which was more painful to him then her death.

WEIGHTY ISSUE

✝

She looked like a chapatti full of hot air, shining with the application of pure desi ghee, exactly like the ones' my mother said indicated that the one for whom it was meant had a healthy appetite. But that was not how it seemed to me for Uncle looked like a leather whip all thin & sinewy.

Hearing us giggle my mother fixed us with a glare, which only meant one thing,' Get out of my sight before I whip you for your impertinence.' Aunty after all was my mother's first cousin & I can now empathize with her for the anger our laughter provoked for they both were very close to each other.

From snippets overheard by eavesdropping on elders' gossip we gathered that Aunty & Uncle had a love marriage, which had scandalized the entire community at that time. He belonged to wealthy family who were erstwhile zamindars. Uncle had sat for the provincial service examinations as per the wishes of his father who was still treated like a zamindar by their village elders.

He was a final year student at the college, when he saw aunty on a monsoon day, stepping out from the rain into the college corridors. Like everyone else he too was standing there waiting for the shower to stop. In those days aunty looked like 'Sadhana' the heroine of yesteryears, her curvaceous figure clad in a hugging polyester kurta, which stuck to her like second skin. All the boys standing in the corridor had heaved a collective sigh but aunty claimed she had eyes only for uncle, who was considered quite a dandy in the college. At this point uncle would usually take over & he would narrate how that one glance cast at him, from under the hair falling over her forehead, like that of Pinky our pet Pomeranian, had all but done him in. Now there would be accusations & corrections about that particular moment by both parties & it got very colorful with each narration.

Anyway cutting a long story short, these looks soon turned into surreptitious meetings behind the banyan tree growing in the college compound. At this particular stage in the gossip everybody gathered would pretend to be scandalized & look at aunty who would glance coquettishly at uncle, behaving like a teenage girl once more.

Letters it seems were exchanged one of which fell into the hands of the *zamindar sahib* who promptly summoned his erring son. It after all involved an inter-caste girl. Uncle stood his ground & stated that he would marry only aunty. He had meanwhile cleared the provincial service examination & would be soon appointed a Deputy Collector. Those we all young ones agreed must have lent him courage to stand up to his father who looked very fearsome if his black & white photographs were anything to go by.

Anyway the svelte missus wed the handsome lad & they traveled from post to post having two children in between till finally they settled in Delhi where uncle held a key post as assistant secretary with Government of India. This is where we came in touch with Uncle & Aunty. Their boys were both bhaiya for us & they were in prestigious colleges following the footsteps of their parents & busy wooing girls of all shapes & sizes.

Now Aunty continued to grow in girth month after month & my mother was always scared about whether the dining room chair would creak under her weight thus embarrassing all of us every time they were expected for lunch. Uncle on the other hand still looked quite handsome. He played tennis regularly at the club & fishing for compliments would stretch his head back & suck in his stomach, a gesture we all were familiar would be followed by the typed phrase 'I am no longer as fit as I once was' to which one of us had to reply 'You look fit as a fiddle or you can give the younger lot a run for their money *etcetera-etcetera*'. He would beam at this & proceed onward without a second glance-leaving aunty fuming inside.

It was not as if she had not tried to reign in the overflowing belly by doing yoga *aasans* or not tried to reduce the rolls of fat on her back, which had a tendency to pour out of her low cut blouses like freshly kneaded dough, by going on Atkins diet but all to no avail. Thousands of rupees had been wasted on the gym & by now she was a well known figure in & around all the gyms in our locality for good marketing means pampering valuable customers especially those who are here to stay.

Aunty confided her weighty despair to my mother who always lent her delicate shoulder & some home remedy to cure the problem. Of late she seemed to be even more overwrought & we heard her confiding in mother that uncle was not paying enough attention to her these days & that had to be because of her massive size. She was contemplating some drastic action now. Mother told her to stop being silly but the tone of her voice suggested she too was not convinced.

Approximately Four months after this particular conversation we all were rudely woken up in the morning by aunty's wailing arrival. "Indu", she hugged my mother, "He has been diagnosed with a cholesterol problem & it is all due to me".

"Come on, how can a health problem be due to you & cholesterol can be controlled" my mother replied, patting her ample back & trying to console her meanwhile trying to retain her balance under the gargantuan weight.

"No, I fed him the pudding & custards & also the small rasogollas which has led to this state" she bemoaned still leaning on my poor mother.

"But he ate it *naa*, so how does that make you alone guilty" reasoned mother.

"He never ate sweets earlier", she sniffled & looking a trifle guilty continued, "it was just to increase his weight too, that I persuaded him to eat my cakes & *jalebis*. He soon developed a taste for them. You know I even took special cookery classes to make all these enticing sweets" & with that she let go another long wail.

We all tried to look solemn while trying to suppress the laughter bubbling within us while tears of remorse rolled down the chubby gleaming cheeks of poor dear aunty.

THE SILENCE
WITHIN—A NARRATIVE

⚓

(Official looking document lying on the small round dining table. A television set showing a cookery show.)

(Glass bowl placed on dining table, lady standing & stirring batter in it. Muttering aloud)

'He has definitely found a replacement else he would not be so persistent. Third summon in a matter of three months. The judicial machinery does not work this fast. He is definitely greasing somebody's hands. Must be really desperate to resort to this. This replacement he has found must be tightening his screw. (pauses from the task at hand, looks up) Why am I using he term replacement, that would imply a substitute or a stand-in. No an accurate term would be alternate because he would now like to live with somebody who is unlike me or would he? We weren't so bad together after all'.

(Addressing the audience)

'Our courtship years were as a matter of fact wonderful. It seems like just yesterday that he was standing quivering in his polished brown shoes in front of the boss's room. I was the dragon lady guarding the citadel while he was the new recruit waiting for introductions to the king. His brown shoes seemed incongruous with the black trousers & white shirt. He was wearing a tasteful blue tie though. Later I learnt, the tie had been a parting gift from his girlfriend. That was him always practical. I could not imagine wearing a gift from someone who had broken my heart to my first interview. To this date I am not sure whether he was too practical or very romantic. He was clutching a man's valise which had seen better days. I had felt distinctly sorry for him'.

'He had introduced himself, 'Siddhartha Singh to meet Agarwal Sir. I am new to this company. Joining today.' He had a voice that reminded me of melting chocolate. I had gone weak in the knees & was grateful that I was sitting behind my desk. I had informed boss him about Siddhartha's arrival but before buzzing him in, I asked 'Which is your alma mater? Upon learning that it was the same as that of boss's son, advised him to harp about it. Fifteen minutes later he had stepped out of the office, beaming. He had thanked me & asked me out for coffe the same evening. Back then I had been living in a working woman's hostel with practically no social life. I had agreed, almost too readily. It was during the evening that he told me about his girlfriend with who he had spent his college years. She had flown off o foreign shores for further studies while he had been forced by his circumstances to stay back & look for a job. They had agreed to call off their relationship & go their separate ways. His wounds were raw & I had just the right balm for it'.

'That was the first of many evening's we spent together. Siddhartha was sharing quarters with two bachelor's and we met at his apartment when the other two were out. Our relationship became the hot topic of gossip in the office. A year later, he left to join another company in the city at a higher position. Our relationship continued even though we could not spend as much time together now. We entered our third year when one day he proposed marriage to me. I belong to a conservative middle class family and like all girls dreamt of marriage and home, I had readily said yes. Our families too had agreed. I took a month long leave from my job which soon extended to another month till i decided to quit. Home was more important than career'.

(Picks up the bowl. Stares at it distastefully)

'I never enjoyed cooking. Siddhartha was a foodie & would continue harping about the various mouth watering dishes his mother prepared. Later I learnt from the old lady that she had been as averse to cooking as I was & given a choice would not enter the kitchen but since she had been required to cook so she decided to do it perfectly. I learnt many recipes from her & also managed a few of my own. Siddhartha actually boasted about my culinary skills to his friends & once I week I prepared lunch for all his office friends on demand. My aversion to cooking never died but

I began to take pride in baking the perfect cake, grilling the softest potatoes & mincing the finest meat'.

We did not have any children & though the doctors could not find anything wrong with either of us still I remained barren. Maybe if we had children, we would have forcibly stayed together. Would such a forced togetherness be better than our current state of separation? I do not know. I will allow this question to hang like all others in the vacuum around me'.

(Goes to the television set, picks up the remote lying on it. Walks back & resumes her seat)

'My marriage proceeded like any other & now twelve years down the lines when I look back I cannot put my finger on that single instance when things began to unravel. We had been like two silk threads braided & forcibly held together by the institution called marriage'.

(Changes channels but finds nothing of interest)

'They will not be airing the 'Single Female traveler' for another fifteen minutes'.

(Switches off the television & turns to the audience)

'Whenever a name is given to a relationship, the parties involved start sub-consciously behaving in a manner, to fit the roles written for the part. The expectations from self & other suddenly rise. The carefree existence is truncated & forceful molding starts taking its place. Striving for the existential things we soon enter a routine that has no place for the unexpected & unpredictable. Monotony seeps into our very being. Back at the house, I remember it was just another ordinary day. I was sitting in my favorite sofa which was placed to catch the last rays of the setting sun. The door of our flat had opened. I was reading some woman's magazine. He had walked in, with his usual haggard expression, house keys in one hand, Tiffin & briefcase in another. Without looking at me he had placed the briefcase on the dining table & walked to the bedroom. Emptiness had begun to creep inside me. It was like a mist which entered through my heart & slowly spread throughout my body till my extremities turned to ice. I felt a hollowness within me which was so empty that I thought I would just collapse within. I don't remember for how long I sat there feeling without but his voice demanding dinner had shaken me out of it. 'Did you see a ghost?' he had jocularly asked. Another distasteful habit of his besides smoking. He never understood that humor had a place & time. I had been forewarned about it during our courtship. It was after one of those office parties where I had all dolled up & was looking pretty good if I may say so. Later when he drove me to the hostel, he parked his bike in a dark corner and we began to neck. He softly started crooning a love song which was actually very romantic. I felt all mushy and told him that if he continued singing to me like this I would have to seriously consider taking up with him for seven life times. He at once removed himself & replied serious faced,' I had better stop then.' Now can you imagine my plight then, tears sprung to my eyes, he was at once apologetic saying that he was just joking but the moment had passed.

Then there was this other time, we were in bed & I was reciting this beautiful poem by Robert Graves, 'I, Love &

you, (he whispers) only I and you'; he interrupted me 'he ultra whispers'. My heart sank with a whoosh. Here I was in the throes of romance and my partner in bliss ruins the moment by cannibalizing the beautiful poetry with reference to a sanitary napkin. Believe me you never forget such instances. I can quote many other moments of this nature but looking at the whole picture it was not about his misplaced humor or my pretentious high faulting ways. We were co-existing, each in our own sphere & it would continue this way indefinitely'.

We were excruciatingly polite with each other & to the outside world we presented a picture of marital bliss & harmony. Our house had turned into a hostel to which both came at the end of the day to catch a few winks. Now two people cannot exist in silence for an extended period despite what they say in the movies. I would sometimes get curious as to his whereabouts & question him about his day to which I got non committal replies. He never asked as to what I did throughout the day. I guess this silence was easy for him in fact it was kind of a relief from his nagging wife. He stepped out of the house everyday & went about his daily work, interacting with people making decisions, working out choices, exchanging banter while on the other hand I had to content with talking to my mother who is no great conversationalist. We did go out for parties but they too had begun to bore me & I took to avoiding them. He would go out without me, always making some excuse about my absence till I came to be regarded by our acquaintances as an invalid surrounded by visiting relatives. I turned into a recluse. The television set was my only companion & before late I knew the schedule of every program on twenty different channels for the entire week. I was going to ruins.

We lived together & grew apart till there was nothing connecting the two of us. The fights that had taken place during our early years had stopped. Now there was just a ghastly silence & that silence was leaching into me'.

'Then one day I packed my bags, left a note stating that I was going to my parent's. There is nothing significant I remember about that day, in fact I do not even remember the date. Back then I had not thought it would be a permanent departure. He had called at my parent's & we had talked, both agreeing that it was good for me that I stay with my parent's for a few days. The days had extended into a couple of month's & my parent's had started worrying. I had applied for a secretarial job at a small firm. I left my parent's house once I got the job & lived in the hostel for a few months. Life had come full circle'.

'This apartment I got on rent through an office colleague. This letter that you see in front of me is a court notice giving the next date for hearing. My husband filed for divorce last month

(pauses)

'No, I don't want to live with him either. We have nothing more to give each other. No, I will not sign the divorce papers though'.

(Addressing the audience forcefully)

'Do you have any idea what stigma it is to live under the tag of Divorced Single woman? It is like you are wearing a 'Come Hither' sign for men. The women folk are no better & eye you suspiciously like you are a Mata Hari on the prowl for their precious husbands. My landlady does not know that I am separated from my husband, neither do my office colleagues. My parents are still wishing & willing me to reconcile with my husband. I do not know how to explain it to them that there is no dispute in the first place that has to be reconciled. A few of my childhood friends are aware of my situation but I have taken to avoiding them too after they took it up in themselves to talk about their own marital discord, drawing parallel with my case & always concluding that the same thing was happening everywhere around with each one of us, so there was no need to throw away my marriage'.

'This line of argument never went down well with me. In my school days I always was good at mathematics because it was logical, equations were matched. Now, because everyone was living through their marriage despite dissonance therefore I too should toe the same line was a very faulty argument. As somebody once said 'The voice of majority is no proof of justice,' moreover the majority was not offering me any proof that they were any happier than me staying in a dead relationship'.

'Well despite all the above arguments I will not give up this black thread around my neck. It offers me a protection which no law does. No don't take me wrong. I do not want to in anyway punish my husband. Truth be told, I did not make him any happier either. I wanted the cushions on the sofa in place at the precise angle at all times, the curtains had to be spread only this much and I actually arrange the cutlery during dinners at restaurants to keep them parallel. It can grate upon the thickest of nerves. Now my husband had a habit of rolling the bed-sheets together while sleeping, somehow he could not or would not lift his mass a bit while turning in his sleep and even when reclining on the bed he would slide his weight down to get comfortable which undid the carefully tucked in corners of the sheet. In the early years of marriage I protested loudly about this. He took it sportingly initially & made light of it but gradually he began to turn a deaf ear & I was left screaming my pent up frustration at a wall. During the latter years I stopped complaining & used to iron the bed-sheet every morning to remove its creases. This time around he began to mock my habit & called me crazy. I know my behavior is obsessive at times but then he could have been just tolerant & let it pass rather than mocking me in front of family & friends'.

'Now I will bid you adieu. It is time for my Pilate classes. When you are alone, you have to follow a routine or the loneliness begins to creep inside. In time I might change my mind about signing the divorce papers. One thing I have learnt and that is life is full of surprises so one should never make any concrete plans for future'.

THE CHATTER
WITHOUT-A NARRATIVE

✠

(Lying on a table are a laptop which is switched on. A half empty beer bottle & a Copy of divorce papers. There are two chairs man is occupying one while thumbing through the papers.)

W hy does she not sign the damn papers & finish what she started? She was the one who decided to quit. I still wonder though, how did she ever arrive at the decision to leave? I mean, I won't deny having similar thoughts but (long pause) . . . . I guess I could never muster the courage to walk out of a ten year old bondage. Never knew she had it in her, to take such a bold step. (Pause) I am beginning to get used to her absence now. It is not easy. After all, I spent one fourth of my lifetime in her constant presence, waking up to her standing with my daily dose of tea, sleeping only after gorging on her delicious dinner under he watchful eye.

She is a mean cook, my wife. That is one thing I really miss, her delicious cooking.

(Puts the a papers aside & draws the laptop towards himself)

Once I began to call for canteen food at the office, my colleagues began to drop hints about my personal life. Obviously I could not tell them, 'Dear friends, no more of chicken curry because your bhabhi has upped & left.' That would show me in such poor light. Every time some nosy colleague asked me about her, I had hummed & hawed. But once I learnt she had taken a job, I dropped hints that all was not well on my personal front. A few more weeks later I confided in a so called friend that I had separated from my wife. I knew the word would spread like fire & it did as was obvious from the murderous glances from my female colleagues & envious looks from my male friends.

(Takes a gulp from the beer and mutters)

'Remembering all these passwords is really becoming troublesome. My wife could really press my keys. We had seven years of togetherness which prepared us for that moment of separation. In fact during the later years my wife had made life really simple for me. Earlier whenever I was late from office, she would quarrel but gradually the quarrels were replaced by a silence which turned deathly'. (Sighs) I took the silence in my stride, there was no point disturbing a dormant volcano. I used to be apprehensive about returning home but as I figured that she would not react, I stopped bothering.(Pause) Maybe I misunderstood her passive silence, but then I was too busy with work & other interests'.

(Looks at the audience)

'No, don't take me wrong all my flirtations were merely platonic. Which man in his right mind will not make a pass at a good-looking girl. Some of them proceeded from coffee to lunch but that was that. Except for that solitary one night stand at Mumbai where I had gone on a business trip, I remained faithful to my marriage, at least physically faithful'.

(Takes out his mobile from the pocket & begins to dial)

'Hello, Jagnnath Sweets, Yes this is Siddhartha calling from D-Block. Namaste, mera order lena. Yes make it paneer with kulchas. Also tell Chotu to get two lager while he is on his way. OK, Thank You'.

(Puts phone in his pocket & continues addressing the audience)

'The spark between us had died & with it had disintegrated the emotional bond holding us together. I really tried to build the bridges between us but she would not support me. She refused to go out to parties with me instead choosing to stay home seething in her cauldron'.

(Gets up stretches himself, stoops in front of laptop & fidgets with the keys)

'Neither of us is to be blamed for this separation. We were simply finished with each other & she had the guts to call it for what it is . . . a dead relation. I am infact grateful to her for having taken this step'.

(Picks up beer bottle, addresses audience)

'She is certainly stronger than me. Had this not happened we would have spent our balance years being polite to each other. Now at least we can each move on, though why she is not signing the divorce papers is a mystery to me'.

(Moves around, kicking a stray piece of clothing out of the way, twisting his wrist)

'The early months of separation were almost a relief. I was not required to confirm to the high standards. I could walk out of the bathroom, naked as the day I was born, scratching my groin. I had the luxury to fart & burp at will after gorging on beer & mutton curry'.

(Leans towards the audience, pointing the beer bottle)

'That smell can put anybody off curry for life. Digging my nose & scratching my armpit while sitting in front of the television are the other treats I am now entitled to.'

(Walks back to table, puts beer bottle on it, stretches his limbs)

'After a while though these extravaganzas also began to bore me. In fact I should tell you that I reverted back to tooting, burping & digging only in the privacy of my washroom though I still enjoy strolling out without a towel around my midriff. It is liberating.'

(Sits down, lifts the beer bottle to check quantity, pulls laptop towards himself)

'I am on half a dozen dating sites now or to be accurate I am now active on these sites. I have always had these accounts, even while I was living with my wife. A guy is allowed his toys. My telephone company is having a ball with the internet bill I am running on these chat rooms. Except for my name I have given all the correct details on the net. In fact every time a female asks about my marital status, I am truthful, I tell her that my wife has walked out on me. It has a very funny effect on them, they at once become concerned & protective, their motherly instinct is aroused & my predatory sense smells it. I went out with a couple of these women but finally decided to stick to chatting with them anonymously. They all wanted to cuddle & in be cuddled. Now I had had enough of cuddling to last me a life time'.

(Suddenly interested in laptop)

'Ah Ha, Samiksha is online, an intelligent person that one.

(Starts typing)

'Hi, how was your trip'?

(Sits back, takes a sip from the beer, addresses audience)

'I found someone, no not Samiksha. I met Maya during training. She was one of the speakers. All of us were mesmerized by her, she has a magnetism that is hard to ignore. I had got the contact details of the consultation firm she was working with & called their office. On my first try I ahead been told that she was out of the city but the next week I had been able to get in touch with her. Our first telephone conversation had been very polite & I had merely praised her oratory skills.'

(Types again)

'Yeah I know the Japs can kill you with their politeness, I have interacted with them but only through video conferencing. I had to spray muscle relaxants on my back after all that bowing'.

(Sits back again & talks to audience)

'I was out of practice & had no idea how to proceed further when a golden opportunity came my way. Our Human resource department was looking to get an employee satisfaction survey done at the local level only & being the HR head in this city it was up to me to decide the name of the firm that would take up the survey. It was obvious, what I had to do. I specifically requested for Maya to undertake the survey & her firm did not disappoint me though I was told, she was much in demand but our price was too lucrative to refuse. After that there was no stopping me. We bumped into each other frequently or should I say I created opportunities to interact with her' *(Types again)*

'You should have practiced saying *Mau takesan desu.* It means 'that's enough'. Maya is all that my wife is not. She has an attitude which shows the finger o the world which we men find very attractive. She is a challenge & whoever conquers her would be the man amongst men'.(Types) Hey Lisa, I would be partial to an avocado salad if you made it dressed only in your frilly apron.

(Takes the last sip from beer, turns it upside down & shakes it)

'Great! My wife was like the girl next door who you introduce to your parents, while Maya is somebody who makes you elope with her just to spite your parents. That element of danger adds to the livewire. In the beginning I was very protective about my wife. She had that fragile quality which made her seem so vulnerable that all my protective instincts were aroused. I wanted to protect her from the big bad world. Slowly I became her focal point of existence which was very endearing in the beginning. Imagine having a human being totally dedicated & committed to your needs. I was her universe which does not mean she did not have a mind of her own. She could be very stubborn when she chose to be especially with regard to my choice of friends. Besides those bouts of obstinacy she was a perfect wife. Too perfect, in fact. I had begun to feel claustrophobic and had on more than one occasion wished she would get a life. (Types) Naughty, come on I am just appreciating your talent like any full blooded male. (Sits back)I had encouraged her to get a job but she had not wanted to, choosing to watch those cookery shows instead & experimenting her learning on me. (Types) Oyasuminasai Samiksha. (Sits back & types again)

Yes, I googled goodnight for Japanese, Bye.'

(Sits back)

'A good girl that one. Now Maya has a spirit & personality that is indomitable. She is a force. On our third date itself I had told her about our separation & for the first time admitted to anyone that it was my wife who had walked out on me. I did not want to start on a false note with Maya. Here was someone special with who I wanted to be completely truthful. Maya had looked at me across the dining table, 'That must have taken guts.'

(Pauses, looks at audience)

'Till date I don't know whether she was referring to my wife or me, I sure hope it was me & that is why I do not ask her. She might flippantly reply that she was referring to my wife even if she was not. That is Maya always keeping you on the edge'.

Door bell rings. 'My food'.

(Walks out, walks back in with a paper bag & two bottles of beer, puts them on the table)

'It has been more than three years that my wife & I separated, three months back I decided to make this legal, after all there was no point continuing something we both did not want. She has not bothered to reply to my earlier two notices so I sent her a third & am hoping she would consent to an amicable settlement. I see no reason why she would not. I want something more permanent with Maya but at the same time I have apprehensions. There is something wild & unbridled about her that attracted me to her in the first place but now I am not so sure. I feel threatened by her energy'.

(Removes a plastic box containing vegetable & foil wrapped chapattis. Begins to un-wrap them then stops. Opens a drawer

*to take out the beer opener & proceeds to open a beer. Takes a
big gulp, all the while standing up)*

'I had bought her a diamond bracelet for her birthday;
she had appreciated it a lot but insisted that I return it as
she did not wear diamonds. She then made me buy her a
dress instead. Two months later on my birthday she bought
me a designer suit which must have cost three times the
dress I had purchased for her. Later we were at this five star
for dinner. We had been sipping on our cocktails when a
distinguished looking man got up from his table & walked
across to us. 'Hello, Gorgeous,' those had been his exact
words. Maya had squealed & jumped out of her seat. They
had hugged in full public view. After this demonstration
of intimacy the introductions had been made. I had been
introduced as a dear friend while he was tagged an old dear
friend. I don't know if I can cope with very many such old
friends, she seems to be having a bevy of them but that is
not the point. I was not intimidated by her large circle of
influential friends or her proximity to them. Maya is a very
loyal girl'.

(Pauses)

'It was what happened after the dinner. Both of us
insisted that Maya's dear old friend join us for dinner with
his companion. They proved to be good company. He was an
investment banker while his friend worked with the airline
industry. They regaled us with anecdotes & we ended up
promising to catch up with each other soon. The maitre de
came with the cheque. Maya signaled him with her eyes to
bring the cheque & before we could protest she had handed
over her credit card. All of us protested, I strongly than

others after all it was my birthday treat. She flipped her head (imitates) & replied, 'It is part of your birthday present;' then she lowered her head suggestively & cooed (mimics), 'I will have my treat later.' Her dear old friend & his companion tittered while I turned red with embarrassment. She had become the provider & initiator of sex thus rendering me redundant. She had taken on the man's job & the man had been made redundant. I felt castrated.

(Types absentmindedly) '

Yes Lisa, I think you are very hot'.

(Sits down, stares vacantly at the laptop)

'A man has his needs. I enjoy being handcuffed to a four poster occasionally but not every time. I should be the hunter gatherer'.

(Shrugs, pulls the food towards himself)

'I will propose to her tomorrow. I am the alpha male'.

LUNCH AND LYNCH

✠

They walked into the canteen carrying an assortment of plastic & jute bags & went to the table they habitually chose. The chairs were pulled up & bags were deposited on the table. The six seated themselves & with reverence started taking out tiffin boxes of varied shapes, sizes & material from the bags in front of them. The canteen attendant came & lay six plates & spoons on the table. 'Get *Chaach*' ordered one of the matrons.

This was a ritual honed with years of practice, the plates were swiftly distributed & the tiffins opened. Each tiffin was passed around with all of them taking a small portion of the cooked vegetable it contained. They stuck to their own *paranthas and chapattis* but their plates resembled those dry fruit gift packs which are divided into multiple compartments having a separate nut in each. Then between bites started the exchange which as a rule continued well past the assigned lunch hour & brooked no interference.

'I don't know what to do with that new girl Sushma. Joshi Madam, I taught her everything she knows & now she has become the boss's favorite. Today, boss actually asked for her to go with him to the meeting with General Manager. I had prepared the papers for the meeting but Sushma portrayed it like she had done all the hard work. It was just this two bit idea she came up about making a PowerPoint presentation instead of the usual notes we presented. She is really getting on my nerves.' Thus opened the conference with the opening note delivered by the wiry Mrs Jha. She was visibly disturbed & there was perspiration on her brow by the time she finished.

'Jha madam, why do you get agitated? She is new to the office & will try to impress people, after all she does not have a husband & children to look after. Wait till she gets married . . . . 'consoled Mrs Panda, pulling a tiffin carrying *dumaloo* towards her. Her gold bangles which she replaced every month jingled & the *dupatta* covering her ample bosom threatened to slip into her over laden plate but she continued nonchalantly.

'Try this stuffed *paneer* roll Mrs. Panda, I just learnt the recipe from my daughter-in-law,' said Mrs. Mani who was stick thin herself. The ulcers in her south Indian stomach did not permit her to eat the savory north Indian food so she indulged herself by watching the ample Mrs. Panda gain one kilogram every month on the mouth watering preparations made by her. Mrs. Panda in turn got her discounts from all the saree stores in Karol bagh when they together went shopping.

'You do your work Madhu,' stated Mrs Joshi somberly, 'the girl will soon learn the ways'. The statement had an ominous ring to it Mrs. Ganguly & Mrs. Ghiya nodded their heads while picking delicately at their plates. Both of them were sidekicks of Madam Joshi who was the unopposed leader of this sextuplet. She was due to retire in a couple of months & had given up any semblance of work she might have till then pretended. Her superiors did not assign her any job & she did of course did not volunteer to do any. Her sole occupation was to manage the affairs of her followers.

'Have you noticed how she dresses? We stick to sarees & suits, after all that is our culture wheras she masquerades in pants & skirts calling them business suits. We all know what business it attracts,' tittering Mrs. Ganguly, lookied at Madam Joshi for approval. She thought she had made a good repartee there, only if Madam Joshi would approve now.

Madam Joshi gave an imperceptible nod which meant she approved & the ding lings could get on with this line of attack.

'They have these fancy degrees under their arms but if you ask them to sit at the table and match a year's memos with the accounts they just run away. Give them well maintained excel tables which they manipulate to throw just any figure. If you ask me this computer technology is even today no match for our manual ledgers,' chimed in Mrs. Ghiya who was an accountant from the old school & was constantly threatened by technology.

'These girls today were born in the computer age & by virtue of that have already stolen a march over us. They have youth & competence in technology, in my opinion Mrs. Jha you should not feel so bad. You have your diligence which nobody can match,; stated the sagacious Mrs. Mani. She had two daughters who had recently completed their management studies & joined the work force. They would come home & tell her horror stories about old witches who harassed them & vampires who were always seeking them out to suck their young souls.

'Mrs. Mani, if the tables are so unevenly balanced then it is only fair that we try to put the equilibrium right.' Stated Madam Joshi with equanimity then without waiting for Mrs Mani to reply turned towards Mrs. Jha & said, 'You should not provide any input to the girl from now on. Let her learn the hard way & if Mr. Shashi asks you to help her you take your own time. Do not hurry in anything, understood.'

'Yes Madam Joshi, I was also thinking about doing exactly that. You know Sushma actually stays back late pretending that she has some work to catch up. I thought she was putting in these extra hours to show herself as a dedicated worker but you know what she told me the other day & this is straight from the horse's mouth. She said that whenever she gets late & misses the office bus, Mr. Shashi gives her a lift home. Now not only does Mr Shashi drop her home but also entertains her on the way by playing *antakshri* with her. She said she was in awe of Mr. Shashi as he knew all the old numbers by heart. I am telling you this kid is not averse to anything to climb the corporate ladder which includes being serenaded by a horny old goat.' completed Mrs Jha with a grim smile.

'Mrs. Jha he used to play *antakshri* with you too whenever you took a lift in his car,' taunted Mrs Panda who had never liked Mrs Jha on account of the fact that she never put on any weight despite anything she ate.

'Mrs. Panda, that Shashi used to sing songs, I never accompanied him, there is a difference,' retorted Mrs Jha with a frown.

'Stop it both of you,' Madam Joshi said, 'if that girl is up to tricks, it is our duty to warn the entire office about her. These philandering ways spoil everybody's reputation specially that of Mr. Shashi. Someone should warn him that Garima is into 'kiss & tell' which is not helping his reputation a wee bit.' Other than Mrs Mani, everybody nodded their heads in agreement.

Two months later they all gathered together at a party thrown o the occasion of Madam Joshi's retirement. The sextuplet was in tears like they were losing a parent. Without her guidance they would all be lost. Everybody gave her a present of their own & when Sushma gifted her a shawl she had crocheted herself, Madam Joshi became visibly perturbed. She hugged Sushma to her ample bosom, 'Take care of yourself & here is an amulet I got from Shirdi. It will ward off evil spirits.' The five *tch-tched* as Madam Joshi tied the amulet around Sushma's thin wrist.

Next day during lunch hour, Mrs Jha dragged Sushma along to join them at their table for lunch. That day they discussed the Madam Joshi & Sushma confirmed that last evening after the party Madam Joshi had been dropped home by none other than Mr. Javeri. Mrs. Panda confirmed that she had heard rumors about the two having had an affair all these years. They continued talking about Madam Joshi till it was an hour past lunch time. Before dispersing, all five cordially invited Sushma to join them at the table for lunch the next day too. She had passed muster the initiation into the 'lunch & lynch' club. The sextuplets were once again complete.

MY ORDINARY TALE

✞

The alarm clock goes off signifying the beginning of another endless day. I can hear the wife pottering about in the kitchen; she does not seem to need a mechanical device to indicate a beginning or an end. Hearing me stir she calls out "*Chai tayar hai*", this has been my wake up call for the past many years without interruption except during the children's summer break when they all pack off to my mother-in-laws place.

I remove myself from the bed & proceed to the bathroom to perform my daily ablution. The red plastic lined mirror above the sink reflects an ordinary brown face with indistinguishable features covered by a thatch of luxuriant peppered hair. I have been teased on innumerable occasions about my mop which many say must be a wig. I run my fingers through the thatch & peer at myself closely hoping to find some redeeming thing in this mask I have been given. I hear the mirror sigh warily at this futile effort, so with a self deprecating smile shared between the two of us I proceed to brush my teeth with the *babool* toothpaste favored by the wife.

Tea has been poured directly into the cream colored cup with a faded rose, one of the two remaining cups from the old crockery set. It has been covered with a saucer, all six of which are intact & now used to serve Parle biscuits to guests. It is already lukewarm & tastes insipid but that is the way I have been having tea for all these many years & anything other then this brew would incite a reaction from me. I open the newspaper & am skimming over the news of one heinous crime after another when the son calls out from behind the paper. "Papa, I need 100 rupees for the school picnic".

"100 rupees but all they do is take you to the city garden & give you some popsicles," I see his face fall & quickly go to the bathroom where my trousers are hanging containing my wallet. "Here take 100 rupees for the school & this here 10 for you," his face lights up & he thanks me before skipping out of the house bag, tiffin, 110 rupees & all. I allow myself a smile for when was the last time I had skipped with glee. I return to my newspaper but give up the effort & decide to go for my bath. The wife is familiar with the routine & is at this very moment preparing both my tiffin & breakfast which today being Thursday would consist of *aloo-methi ki sabji* and *tuar ki daal* which would also be served for dinner. Breakfast would be jam bread.

I hurry through my bath & eat my breakfast with a speed which had the boss seen would have definitely invited a comment from him, "I wish you would finish your work too this soon Mister." The wife dressed up in her once blue cotton gown which has now given way to an off-white colour after being repeatedly subjected to detergent puts the tiffin box on the plastic sheet covering our dining table. The plastic sheet is a recent purchase though its purpose on our twelve year old dining table is lost on me.

Lugging my old VIP briefcase, which too is as nondescript as me & carrying my tiffin box in the other hand I call out to the wife's voluptuous back as she proceeds to the kitchen, "Jaa raha hoon."

"*Accha, theek se jaana*", she called out like she had done for every day of our life together though the tone had changed from one of concern to the one now uttered by rote.

I walk to the bus-stand & take my routine 345 number bus. The passengers are all too familiar & so is the mixed odor of Brahmi oil, Lux soap, evil-smelling cheap after-shave. We acknowledge each other with nods, after all having traveled together though with different destinations in mind this curtsy is called for on account of the social-animal status bestowed upon us. Getting down at my office I proceed to my ordinary cubicle a small board on which proclaims the resident of this cabin as Accounts Manager in this tyre company. The Manager had been added after the company head read somewhere, that titles boosted employee morale. It had failed to do so in my case so far. I look at my small work table overloaded with memos, notes & bills. I would eventually have to plough through them but first I have to report to my boss who went under the head Senior Accounts Manager which should logically have made me Junior Accounts Manager but the Junior had not been prefixed as it would have sounded too condescending & lowly & for this

I was eternally grateful. At the age of 43 being referred to as junior would have plummeted my already low self esteem, to the ocean floor. My olfactory glands have meanwhile switched to the vulcanized rubber mode & the cloying smell omnipresent on account of the storage point being situated in the basement filters into my being.

I inhale deeply acclimatizing to the change then tap on the door of Senior Accounts Manager walking in after hearing his gruff "*Aa jao.*" He looks up from whatever he was doing & shifts a few more files towards me which meant I was to run through them too, then went back to his doodling which meant 'Get out you moron.'

Loaded with the files I plod back to the tiny space called my cubicle & proceeded to plough through the numerous papers. After finishing with each I put them in the out-tray which the only office peon would clear during lunch time. Slowly the number of papers begins to reduce & the small desk breaths a bit easy, when quickly the lunch hour is upon us. This as per instruction of super boss had to be a communal activity so all of us at the strike of one trot to the small hall which doubled as our conference hall & dining room. We all open our tiffin boxes at the count of three & proceed to munch on our food resembling a well honed drill in progress. Soon this exercise is over & we rise together in tandem at the sound of a silent gong, proceeding in tandem to the toilets & drinking fountain. This is one place where we relieve & feel relieved exchanging small banter which adds a small temporary sparkle after which it is back to the grind.

The small desk is again groaning under the weight of even more paper then I had managed to clear, but this was nothing new. I sit down with the singular thought in mind, 'Another 4 hours & it would be over.' After lunch I always diligently keep track of time which seems to pass ever so slowly. At around 4 the sour faced lady from across the street would come with her tea kettle & glasses, placing one in front of each one of us noncommittally & moving on. Once long back I had tried to strike up a conversation with her at which she had glared at me so balefully that I had since retreated into my shell.

At four walks in a young girl who we were informed by the only peon is the sour faced lady's daughter. She would now on be coming in place of her mother as the lady had met with an accident & was bed-ridden for good. I feel sorry & decided to help the girl. When she comes to my desk I extended a 50rupees note to her. She stops pouring tea into my glass & looks up. It is a wise gaze penetrating my conscience which I must say is not too clean. I hurriedly state, "*Tumhari amma ke ilaj ke liye.*" She still continues to stare but then the cowardice in my glance convinces her & she accepts the money. I could fathom that look but it was not something I wanted to waste my sleep over, so I decide to relegate it to the dark corners of my conscience from which it would not surface even in my dreams.

Another hour passes & then another. It is time to go home. I wait with the colleagues for our respective buses & am soon on my way home. The smell of *heeng* tells me I have arrived home. The wife has tea steaming on the other burner so after putting the tiffin box in the kitchen I proceed to wash & change clothes. The son is sitting on the dining table doing his homework when I step out. I take the tea from the kitchen and it wait for it to turn lukewarm.

"Papa, I cannot do this algebra sum," the son states handing me the text book & his notebook turned to the last page so that I solve the sum there which he would then diligently copy. I look at the sum then began to explain it to him. He nods all the while & I hope he understands what I am telling him. He is an average student as was expected from his genes.

I finish my tea & switch on the television set for the evening news which carries the same headlines as the morning paper with a change in profile of the dead. I surf through the channels when my wife comes & sits down beside me for it is time for her favorite serials which run neck to neck for an hour & half. I concede the remote to her wondering not for the first time whether these serials were aired precisely at this hour to make households erupt with disharmony or the wife chose to watch these particular ones to grate on my nerves. But then such meandering never lead anywhere so I again pick up the morning paper & wait for the advertisement breaks during which she would go to the kitchen. An hour & half later it is time for dinner so the son who meanwhile has also shifted his position on the dining table to watch the idiot box removes his books & I move to the dining table. The *tuar dal* is there though heated up & there is *aloo matar* which would be re-used in tomorrow's breakfast sandwiches.

Conversation centers on money required for the household & the son's education peppered by a bit of local gossip about the neighbors teenage daughter who is supposedly having a torrid affair with her college friend who had again come to drop her home on his huge motorbike today. The son listens on & I am sure would be reporting back to the neighbors daughter whom he called didi & who kept him fed with chocolates.

Dinner over it is time for bed & after staying a bit longer for some late night news I go to the bedroom followed a bit later by the wife. I turn to embrace her & she shrugs, "It is the time of the month". I *tcch-tcch* expressing sympathy then turn around and try to sleep.

Tomorrow it will begin all over again.

OBITUARY

✟

——————— ✟ ———————

That dastardly phone call was the beginning of the chain reaction, which was now fission out of control. My Uncle had been quietly enjoying his retirement for two years now with daily morning walks three hours dedicated to five different newspapers, helping out my aunt, his wife of thirty-seven years with odd jobs which he now knew required a lot of time & planning. Take for example the topping up of diesel genset, a task he learnt existed only when electricity failed on that hot May afternoon & he had been forced to step out into the inferno with a jerry can to get the stupid machine to start.

But that phone call had ruffled his almost calm existence. The call had been placed by his friend's son reporting that his father had died due to a coronary attack. Uncle had tried to mumble the right words but had found himself faltering in mid-sentence. His brain search engine brought out the memories from college days when life had looked like a cakewalk. Those had been the days of bell-bottom trousers

& shoulder length hair cuts. His now late friend had then been one of the hippy guys around & had generally been acknowledged the best looking dude of their batch. Even now he just had to shut his eyes to remember him strutting about in the boxing ring showing off his well toned body to the combined sighs of his female following. He had been a good sportsman too & his talent in the boxing ring had been legendary.

The health magazines always stated that an active lifestyle reduced the risk of coronary disease & his friend had been everything but a couch potato. Just last month he had participated in a marathon & had even got a decent position. There was no history of heart ailments, which ruled out genetic predisposition so that left only one option age.

Now this selection by elimination had perturbed him immensely. After getting back from the funeral Uncle made an appointment with his doctor for a thorough check up including all the tests one could think off. While waiting for his test results he had tried to immerse himself in his newspapers & daily chores but to no avail. The words would swim in front of his eyes & he was sure he had developed some serious eye ailment or even worse his brain was failing him.

Walking to the bazaar he stumbled on a raised manhole & stepped on some dog poop; things which he had maneuvered around deftly now seemed to be playing tricks with him. During the next few days he managed to hit his shin, bruise his knee & develop an irritating tick which made him repeatedly blink his eyes for clearing his vision.

Aunty became anxious at all these symptoms being put on exhibition by her level headed husband. He urged in fact pleaded with her to accompany him to the doctor's for his test result. The doctor was an old friend & he greeted them with their usual tea cups.

'Can I take sugar in my tea?' he asked, upon which the doctor looked at him with a bemused expression & replied 'Of Course', but with that decided to keep his council till he had spoken to the better half.

'Well, my reports, are they in?' he asked putting his still half full tea cup back on the saucer & pushing it away from himself as if it held some horribly infectious disease.

'Yes they are back & for your age you are healthy as an ox' replied the doctor with a smile.

'My age! Now what does that mean?'

"It means, all your test results are within the limits prescribed for the fifty to seventy year old age bracket & you should continue doing whatever it is that you are doing which keeps you so healthy.'

'So you mean to say my cholesterol, blood pressure, sugar all are in control' he asked with a relieved expression.

'That is exactly what I said old chap. On the side of caution though take up some physical activity & yoga to maintain this healthy existence.'

'Ahem! I have heard that the chances of one catching some lifestyle disease like heart attack increase with age. Is that true?'

'Yes, it most certainly is that is why I am asking you to take up some for of exercise.'

'Thank You. We will take your leave now'; he nudged his wife who was sitting unprepared & she got up with a start. Usually Uncle would linger on with some idle chitchat, which both the doctor & patient enjoyed. He would also extend an invitation to visit them at their home which the doctor would accept but never follow through.

Today though it was different, there was no small talk & the invitation never came forward so she decided to step in & keep up the tradition. 'Please come to visit us sometime with your wife.'

The doctor was both too polite & too seasoned to not understand what was transpiring. He replied gravely 'Someday definitely.'

They both walked back to the car & in silence drove to the house. From then on he took to taking long morning walks, spending an hour playing tennis at the local club & in the evening after dinner went out for a languid stroll with aunty. He mastered the Internet & browsed all sites relating to health & hygiene; in the process becoming a Mister know all in the field of medicine. His medical book purchases would put any final year medical intern to shame.

He would put his newly acquired knowledge to use on himself & pronounce every ache & pain in his body as relating to symptoms of some serious disease. His family GP soon grew tired of the constant hammering & finally put his foot down, when he was woken up in the middle of night by a phone call from his erudite patient who claimed to be suffering from a heart attack at that very moment. An ambulance was rushed to his home & he was admitted into the emergency room where the ECG came out negative & one loud belch from the reclining patient which made the room stink with fermented mutton curry pronounced the verdict: heart burn.

The doctor refused to have anything to do with him so he now decided to get in touch with fellow sufferers who could be found in the daily obituary column. Now these dastardly newspapers always reported the date of demise but never that of birth unless it was a young one who had been called to the heavenly abode before his time.

He would therefore carefully analyze the overhead photograph for wrinkles & gray hair, which would put the deceased in his age bracket. Then he would go to attend the prayer meeting held in his/her memory. After the meeting he would linger on & casually enquire from on of the attendees about the cause of death. A specific illness continuing for a long time did not perturb him but if someone nonchalantly stated that the late so & so had gone of to sleep from which he never woke up or that he had a stroke & never left the ICU alive or that he suddenly fell down gasping & his eyes rolled over before anyone could understand then he became immensely agitated.

That night & for many nights thereafter he would lie awake tossing & turning, consulting his medical books & the internet forums during the day & generally making a nuisance of himself.

Aunty was at her wit's end & persuaded him to join the 'Art of Living' course where he could learn to channelise his energies & be of some use to the society in general. He followed her advice & brought many books relating to yoga & meditation. He joined the weeklong course too but his inner agitation did not calm down. He already knew that death was certain & one should make the most of life, which was what those preachers talked about anyway.

Then one-day things changed. A school bus carrying first & second standard students to the nearby lake for a school picnic had overturned which had made national headlines. More than thirty young children aged between six to eight years died in that freak accident. Their usually quiet town was enraged with the school & city administration. Compensation packages were promised but there was no consoling the grieving parents. That day all the five newspapers were carrying blown up photographs of the accident.

Uncle read the news with a steely heart and turned to page two to follow his daily ritual whereupon waited the shock. It was covered with young smiling faces that had barely lived. The ink setter's worst effort could not diminish the simple innocence of the faces. They looked to be posing for their school magazine announcing their achievements.

They would never be able to fulfill their promises. A sudden brake had sealed their fate. He felt a terrible pall come upon himself. On the third day of the accident he went to the city hall where a condolence meet had been organized for all these young lives.

He went there to relieve some of the terrible grief that had overcome him. In all these three days he had stopped thinking about himself. He found parents & grandparents, uncles & cousins moving around like zombies. The atmosphere was somber then usual but there was no wailing or sobbing. It was as if everyone had unanimously decided to put a lid on their emotions. They were like pressure vessels simmering with grief.

Suddenly a hush fell over the gathering. A very frail looking man was rolled into the hall. He picked up some rose petals & put them in front of the pictures as homage to the lost lives. Somebody whispered that he lived in the city all alone. He had lost his entire family in an accident & was a landmark in our city. He could be spotted at the hospitals & schools involved in one charity or the other & the city folk had immense respect for him.

A hush fell on the crowd over which we all heard his quiet whisper, 'Take care of yourselves, I will join you soon.'

That was the last of my Uncle's self involved, home grown pity.